COLD WAR
IN HELL

COLD WAR IN HELL

HARRY BLAMIRES

Thomas Nelson Publishers
Nashville • Camden • New York

Published in Nashville, Tennessee,
by Thomas Nelson, Inc. and
distributed in Canada
by Lawson Falle, Ltd.,
Cambridge, Ontario.

Printed in the United States of America.

Library of Congress Cataloging in Publication Data

Blamires, Harry.
  Cold war in hell.

  Originally published: London; New York: Longman,
Green, 1955.
  I. Title.
PS3503.L39C6   1984   813'.54   84-16711
ISBN 0-8407-5930-4

CONTENTS

To
my wife

Foreword to edition of 1984

Having conducted my narrator in *The Devil's Hunting Grounds* on a tour of regions which might roughly be called purgatorial, in that they are inhabited neither by the truly saved nor the as yet irreparably damned, it was natural that I should want to take him on a trip to Hell. The trouble about trips to Hell is that, strictly speaking, Hell is not a place from which anyone can come back to tell his tale. Indeed the *Times Literary Supplement* somewhat solemnly declared of my book: "The suggestion (made purely for purposes of allegory) that damnation may not be final is theologically and psychologically misleading." But a more careful reader than the reviewer would discover that no such suggestion is encouraged by the book. The only person who gets out of Hell is the person who has not yet been condemned to go there. True, the angel concedes that a person who really tried to get out of Hell would indeed get out, but the irony is that no inhabitant of Hell would ever be capable of so trying. In finally opting for Hell, one abandons the capacity even to seek salvation.

Representation of life in Hell of course offers rich opportunities for satire of contemporary anti-Christian ways of thinking. It also offers plenty of opportunities for pin-pointing where fashionable trends in contemporary life verge on the diabolical. A good deal of the book is concerned with what goes on in Hell's university, inside Hell's books, at a floor show in Hell, and even in its governing council chamber.

The serious emphasis in *The Devil's Hunting Grounds* was on the contrast between true Christian faith and various forms of evasive pseudo-religion. The serious emphasis in *Cold War in Hell* is upon the need for Christian obedience in the face of fashions and philosophies that ensnare with calls to self-centredness and self-indulgence.

Enemies of Christianity in our age have tried to suggest that obedient acceptance of the faith is a kind of undignified surrender of "freedom of thought." I took the risk in this book therefore of ironically pushing this notion to its logical conclusion, making the devils in Hell disparage Heaven as a totalitarian state sustained by tyrannous brainwashing. In this I was only copying Milton whose devils declare that it is better to reign "freely" in Hell than to serve a tyrant obediently in Heaven—better to live in your own way than to accept God's law and live in His way.

C.S. Lewis made one major criticism of this book which will delight his admirers. He complained that during the conversation between the narrator and the angel in the opening chapter, I had misled readers about the time at which English pubs open on Sundays.

Introduction

The preternatural organisation, whose activities are touched upon during the course of the following narrative, is unfortunately not fictitious. Nor, I regret to say, can my own personal involvement in its intrigues, here recorded, be accounted imaginary. Nevertheless I cannot vouch for the strict accuracy of impressions accumulated during an experience of considerable personal perplexity and even distress.

Some of the characters owing allegiance to His Eminence pass comments which contain offensive references to certain Real Persons. It may be assumed that all such references are intentional and wholly malicious.

Ch'assolver non si può chi non si pente,
nè pentere e volere insieme puossi,
per la contradizion che nol consente.

DANTE: *Inferno*

The Problem Child

How could men be reasonable beings if they had no
knowledge of the Word and Reason of the Father,
through Whom they had received their being?

St. Athanasius: *De Incarnatione*

I had to sprint for the last half mile in order to catch
my train, and I felt sticky and uncomfortable as I began to walk along the corridors in search of a seat.
Good fortune directed me to a compartment with
only one occupant—a smoker too. Soon I was seated
in a corner seat, diagonally opposite a dark-suited
gentleman who was reading a book with evident concentration. I leaned back, exhausted with my exercise,
and the train jerked into motion.

For a few moments I sat with closed eyes, breathing
deeply and thanking my lucky stars that I had caught
the train. When I opened my eyes again, they lighted
upon what seemed to me to be the pleasantest spectacle they had ever seen. Here indeed was a dream come
true! In the ordinary course of my life, on a very ordinary Sunday, I had got on an utterly ordinary train.
Haphazardly I had chosen my compartment from a
hundred others, and here before me sat an unknown
man reading—and reading one of my own books! Yes,
there he sat, reading my own work, as though it were
the most ordinary thing in the world to do. Only a
writer knows what that means. To read a favourable
review of one's book is a pleasurable experience: to re-

ceive an enthusiastic letter of approval from a pleased reader is perhaps even more agreeable. But what are these calculated tributes to authorship compared to the thrill of discovering a stranger, casually encountered in the humdrum career of daily life, reading one's book as naturally and shamelessly as if he were reading Shakespeare or T. S. Eliot?

I began to examine the stranger more closely. He looked very intelligent, I thought; and the way he concentrated on the book, without regard to me or to his surroundings, suggested that he was an earnest, studious type, probably not much given to flippancy or bonhomie. He wore a dark hat and the rim was turned down so that I could not see his eyes, but there was a dignity about his uprightness as he sat there with the book held vertically on his knees. The continued silence and stillness of the man increased my already kindled respect for him.

Naturally I felt the urge to introduce myself. But how to do it delicately? How achieve the casualness which would kill any appearance of vanity or self-display? I did not know; so I just cleared my throat noisily and hoped for the best. But the stranger only turned a page without raising his head. Wisely I rejected the plan of remarking that the book appeared to be very interesting. Instead I cleared my throat again, this time more noisily and portentously, and I drew in my breath with an impressive sigh. Then indeed he spoke.

"Are you about to make a speech?"

Slowly and deliberately he closed the book, lifted his head, removed his hat and looked me in the eyes. I jumped from the seat in utter astonishment.

"Lamiel!" I gasped.

"Your Guardian Angel," he replied, "come to pay

you a brief visit; not entirely informal and yet, on the other hand, not devastatingly official. You may sit and be at ease. No violent cataclysm is at hand. It is true that I represent something of an eruption in the natural course of events: but I tried to ease the shock. You were surely prepared for something extraordinary, when you chanced upon a stranger reading your book?"

A little ruefully I sank back into the corner and tried to calm myself; for my hands were trembling and even my legs would not keep still. Only half in control of myself, I blurted out a silly question.

"What on earth are you doing here?"

"What am I doing here on earth, you mean to ask, I believe. I have already told you that I have come to visit you."

"Yes, but why? What have I done?"

"You have done nothing—nothing worth speaking of, that is. *I* am the one who has done something. I have come to visit you on your home ground."

"But why should *I* be visited...?"

Lamiel raised his hand with an authoritative gesture, and the hint of a smile creased his cheeks.

"You are in danger of misunderstanding the situation from the outset," he said. "I have been sent here, but *you* are not the cause. You must not begin to picture yourself as the hero of an action which has set the Hosts of Heaven in motion. For all that you have done, we might still have been at our wonted tasks."

I began to feel more comfortable.

"That's a relief," I said.

"You will need it. It is sufficient burden for you that you are to have a visiting angel on your hands for a few days."

I realised that it was. All kinds of practical problems rushed to mind. How was I to introduce him to people; how explain him away?"

"You won't need to explain me away," he said, reading my thoughts. "I travel *incognito* so far as unbelievers are concerned. That follows inevitably from their unbelief. Others will see me and will understand. You will find that normality will not be unduly disturbed. I can promise you that I shall not embarrass you by disappearing in full daylight or by flying from one story to another. I shall make use of staircases like the rest of you, and do my best to fit in with the finite limitations obtaining here-abouts for human beings. *No superfluous conjuring tricks* was the Order of the Day given to us, and it must govern my operations. You will admit that my present appearance is not likely to astonish anyone. It will scarcely provide the journalists with new proof of the supernatural."

"You look like a perfectly ordinary parson," I agreed.

"Yes," he said, reflectively fingering his clerical collar. "I thought this a desirable safeguard. I know something of your environment. One is likely to be considered extremely odd if one speaks on religious subjects with out this projection. It is an added device for saving us both from embarrassment. Besides, wearing this, no one will ask me what I do for a living."

I could think of dozens of even more awkward questions which might be asked: but I realised that Lamiel was going to do his best to fit in, and for that I was very grateful. Perhaps it wouldn't be too bad, if he remained in his present mood.

"You must endeavour to see the funny side of things," he went on. "Frankly I believe the experience

will be enjoyable for both of us. But you will spoil it,
for yourself at any rate, if you spend your time in a
state of nervous tension, continually waiting for me to
turn all gold or vanish in a vaporous mist. I have given
you my word that I intend to play the game. Of
course, I cannot give any absolute guarantee against
possible lapses in moments of extreme displeasure or
delight, but, accidents apart, there will be no aero-
nautics and no untoward combustion. Your house will
smoke only from the chimneys, in the usual manner.
By the way, you might as well have this."

He handed me my own book.

"It wasn't legally acquired, I'm afraid. I didn't buy
it. I searched numerous bookstalls without being able
to find a copy. So I just arranged something. We are,
after all, allowed considerable latitude over the inter-
pretation of the word *superfluous*. It was my only
lapse so far."

"You might as well keep it," I said.

"That's very kind of you. I will.... Though it isn't
wholly to my taste," he added, flicking over the pages
and nodding reflectively. Then he suddenly slapped
the book shut and threw it down on the seat.

"I tantalise you unnecessarily. You want to know
why I'm here."

Of course I did. There was no cause for me to
speak. I waited for Lamiel to plunge into his story.

"You must pardon a brief excursion into heavenly
politics," he said. "It is a necessary preliminary to
what I have to tell you. I must explain that the Hierarchies above have, like you, their controversies over
questions of policy. At present there is grave dispute
over the question how we ought to cater for the twentieth century. It is our problem century, for twentieth-

century man is our problem child. You must
understand that I am not referring to the moral delinquency in you and your contemporaries. It isn't this
that troubles us; for though the delinquency is important it presents no *special* problem. You see, men of all
centuries are delinquents. Morally, twentieth-century
man presents the same spectacle as his forebears and, I
may add, as his successors. No, it's the odd state of
mind into which he has fallen that disquiets us. His in-
tellect is corrupted in a fashion quite without prece-
dent. In a word, twentieth-century man is *irrational*.
That is what makes him our problem child."

"But I'm astonished to hear you say that," I said. "I
always understood that modern man suffers from a
deficiency of faith—that he is in danger of being *too*
rational. Surely this is the age of Science...."

"A moment, please. You have already compressed
so much confusion of thought into a single sentence as
to provide me with material for an hour's discussion.
To begin with, the implied antithesis between faith
and reason just will not do. It is reason which guides
man to pass judgments upon human life and its limitations; and, having judged, he finds the venture of
faith absolutely indispensable. It is reason which en-
ables you to distinguish the good from the bad, the
beautiful from the ugly, the true from the false. Faith
is obedience and self-committal. Reason distinguishes
and preserves the values and standards which can call
obedience and self-committal into play. If reason does
not fulfil its proper function, then the moral will is deprived of any sense of direction."

"It sounds terribly difficult," I said.

"Then let me put it more simply. Suppose this compartment were to fill up at the next station, so that

people were standing in the corridors; and a hopeful woman, with a baby in her arms, chose to stand outside this door. Now the mysterious voice within you, which you call conscience, urges you to observe a certain code in your behaviour to others; but it is reason which tells you exactly what that code is and how it applies to the immediate situation. Reason explains to you your particular obligations to a woman standing in a train with a baby in her arms. It reminds you that, as a young and healthy man, you have no excuse for neglecting your obligations. In short, reason tells you that it is good that you should give her your seat, bad that you should stick to it. Then the moral will comes into play. You actually do what is good—or what is bad. In either case it is by virtue of your reason that you know what you are doing. Now whether you are a good man is determined by what you do: whether you are a rational man is decided, in the first place, by what you know. Of course only the good man is strictly rational in the last analysis, since it is highly irrational to do what reason tells you is bad. Nevertheless, I think you can see my point. If the reason is corrupted, it becomes increasingly difficult for men to be good."

"You use the word *reason* in an unfamiliar way," I said.

"The fact that it is unfamiliar proves my point. You are losing your hold on true reason. This, in brief, is the plight of your modern world. You think that the exercise of reason is simply a matter of weighing, measuring and recording. You think that you are at your most rational when you say, 'My drawing-room is eighteen feet by twelve feet' or 'Metals expand when heated.' But don't you see that judgments of this kind are wholly rooted in the limited sphere of earthly experience?"

"None the less true," I said.

"No doubt. But the proper exercise of reason consists in rising above your earthly experience, and passing judgment upon it in the light of certain values which transcend the finite order. Man is supremely rational when he says, 'This action is good' or 'This statue is beautiful'—for he then judges his environment in terms of a higher order discerned by his reason. Your generation systematically neglects the existence of this higher order: in so doing it destroys the foundations for judgments of value. If you want to know whether a thing is good, you no longer consult your God-given reason. You take a majority vote by Gallup Poll. In denying reason its proper sphere of operation, your contemporaries corrupt the very faculty they pretend to serve. And we arrive at the shocking stage of confusion exemplified in your own observation—the idea that modern man suffers from an excess of reason."

"You mean," I said, "that in fact we suffer from a defect of reason, and confuse the issue by pretending to be especially rational."

"Exactly. That is what makes you our problem children. Men of all centuries have been disobedient and depraved. But usually they have known what laws they were disobeying and by what standards they were depraved. Twentieth-century man has no such knowledge. He is fleeing headlong from reason, and at the same time is claiming an excess of rationality."

"So you have come to make us more rational?"

"Oh, dear, no. You forget how my story began. I referred to a dispute over heavenly policy. The question how to cater for our twentieth-century problem-children has given rise to a controversy among the Hierarchies of an unusually acute kind. We all recognise that you are slaves of Nature in a quite exceptionally ugly way. I don't mean that you propitiate natural deities by formal sacrifices and bow the knee to the sun and moon. That sort of thing is bad enough, but it has a kind of dignity which your prevalent attitude lacks. For you worship Nature with a strange unintentional whole-heartedness, scarcely aware of what you are doing."

"In what way?" I asked.

"You treat the earthly order as the be-all and the end-all. You assume that truth and knowledge are to be obtained only by observation of nature's behaviour, either when left to herself or when plundered for your factories and laboratories.

"How are we to wean you from this drab, thoughtless Pantheism? This question engenders heat amongst us. We have long adopted a policy of Minimum Overt Intervention in human affairs. That is to say, we are not in the habit of appearing to men, either in their dreams or in their waking hours. We do not intrude. We speak only when spoken to. Now a considerable body of angelic opinion holds that the policy of Minimum Overt Intervention is not meeting the present situation. Of late the attack upon the policy has increased. Some of the opponents represent only a small minority. Those are extremists, like the Maximum Interventionists and the Miracle-Mongers. But a growing body of quite moderate opinion now holds that the so-called Non-Intervention Policy ought to be modified. They have a strong case. How can men reach out to a Supernatural Order of whose very existence they are wholly ignorant? That is their cry. And it cannot be ignored."

"It sounds a most cogent case," I said. "For indeed a few instances, which gave evidence of the Supernatural Order, would make an enormous impression upon our generation. The religious situation would be transformed at a stroke."

"There is, however, another side to the question," Lamiel went on. "The policy of Minimum Overt Intervention has its peculiar advantages, as well as its disadvantages. In losing awareness of the Supernatural, man has also lost all sense of the Preternatural—the Subnatural, if you like."

"You mean that we no longer believe in ghosts?"

"No, I mean that you no longer believe in devils. You have ceased to conjure up evil spirits. Black masses are out of fashion. Necromancy is a dying art, and witch-craft has become a joke. This has produced an ironical state of affairs. For some of the devils in Hell are even more unhappy about the situation than are the angels in Heaven."

"Which surely justifies the present policy."

"Wait a moment. There is a subtle difference between the displeasure of the angels and the displeasure of the devils. The angels are upset because their policy does not appear to be bringing the right results. They are upset because man is worshipping nature and rejecting the Supernatural. But the devils have no logical reason to be displeased at this. Men are being weaned from true worship: men are ignoring God. That ought to suit the devils perfectly, if they were consistent. But they are not consistent: they are annoyed because they too are being ignored. All goes well with their primary design of corrupting man; but they resent the fact that man's corrupted soul turns to the worship of Nature instead of to the direct worship of themselves. This is stupid of them, for they never pretended to have any positive design—only the negative design of turning men from God. If they were logical creatures, they would be content with their large measure of contemporary success. But they are not logical. They are envious. They don't want Nature worshipped by man. There is too much good in Nature. It is dangerous, in their eyes, for men to serve the objective order of Nature. Such objective service can so easily be transfigured and redeemed."

"I don't understand," I said.

"It is not very difficult. If a man spends all his time thinking about aeroplanes or television, that is bad from the angelic point of view. These things become idolatries—finite, earthly idolatries, which usurp the place of God, and confine man's vision and pursuits to the worldly level. But the devils are not content with this degree of human perversion. They want to see man's attention focused exclusively upon himself—for self-centredness is the root of all devil-worship. Now, you see, it is easy for these earthly idolatries to lead to completely self-centred worldliness—and therein lies their danger, in our eyes. But it is also possible for these interests in the objective order to nourish a man in service and self-committal to what is other. And that, of course, is the beginning of faith and worship."

"So our plight is not so parlous after all?"

"I'm afraid it is. We must face the facts. The interests and pursuits of twentieth-century men are not, generally speaking, leading them either to worship or to faith. They are nourishing a philosophy and practice of materialistic progress which ultimately serves nothing higher than man's crudest bodily appetites. This progress might lead otherwise, were it accompanied by a keen sense of the values which civilised men ought to serve and the moral precepts which they ought to obey. But progress has bred a passion for power and a lust for ease which corrupt the reason, till it finds its only values in the very idolatries natural man has created. There, in this fact of your irrationality, lie our problem and the root of our angelic controversy."

"Which has brought you here."

"Yes. The demand for modification of our Minimum Overt Intervention Policy led to an extraordinary decision at our last Hierarchical Conclave. Under Seraphic authority a Commission was set up to consider the advantages of increased overt angelic intervention in human affairs. A few of us have been despatched to earth in the capacity of observers. This is not in itself a move towards interventionism. Our duty is merely to spend a few days in human guise and then to report back our findings to the Commission. It is an exciting embassy. We have the right to introduce ourselves to our wards; but there is no likelihood that we shall cause a general stir. Since we are wholly disguised as men, we shall not give rise to anything sensational. The climate of opinion being what it is, people would only make themselves ridiculous by claiming us for supernatural beings."

"I'm quite sure you are right about that," I said. "But what do you expect to gain from your mission?"

"That is not for me to say. I am acting under orders."

"You surely have your own views about what ought to be recommended."

"In my present capacity, it is not my business to

have views on that subject. I was sent to observe. It is my duty to obey."

"Yet you must have some general idea about what you are looking for."

"We want to see human irrationality from the human side. We know it, in all its flaming absurdity, from the angelic side. We want to get the *feel* of it down here. Above all, we want to try to understand why Naturalism should so easily enslave man. We understand man's moral weakness before his own appetites and lusts; but we don't fully understand the mental aberration which makes him say of the finite order—This is all: here is the only truth: by weighing and measuring we record the nature of reality: all else is idle dreams.

"You see, in serving his own lusts, man pursues something in which there is an element of good. But in rejecting the whole idea of the Supernatural Order, he acts in a way which is utterly negative. He belittles himself, injures his status, damages his dignity—and all to no purpose whatsoever. We could understand the rogue of former days who said—'I will have a thoroughly selfish time and then repent and be absolved on my deathbed.' That line was wicked and perilous, petty and short-sighted. But it did give God the credit for being able to save at the last. And it preserved some shreds of spiritual dignity for man. But this denial of Supernature, this perverse sincerity of root-and-branch rejection, this earnestly irrational underestimation of man's origin and his destiny—it is so pitiably self-destructive as to fill us with dismay. Modern man cannot even rise to the dignity of blasphemy. He has left himself with nothing to blaspheme."

"It is a shock," I said, "to hear modern man compared so unfavourably with his predecessors."

"The fact that it comes to you as a shock," said Lamiel, "is what makes it most shocking. Men of previous centuries came to Judgment and bowed to the
recital of their offences. 'Yes,' they admitted, 'I sinned
against charity, against truth, against chastity, against
courage. Yes, I followed my own lusts, making no attempt to keep the law. I made my own earth-bound
will my only divinity. I never hearkened to what
might be God's will for me.' But twentieth-century
men come to Judgment and refuse to bow. When con-
fronted with the tale of their offences—their worldliness, lust, and pride—they stand and shout back
incomprehensible nonsense. 'I was sincere,' they cry. 'I
was true to myself: I expressed my own individuality
without distorting or inhibiting the vital growth
within me. I was loyal to the canons of scientific
thought: I never accepted any fact which could not be
demonstrably verified: I freed my mind from the fetters of tradition and the chains of superstitious
dogma.'

"Of course it is impossible to bring home to such
cases the simple elementary reality of their mean-
nesses, dishonesties, vanities, and adulteries. Some of
our courts have gone so far as to abandon the age-old
practice of always returning a verdict of *Guilty* and
adding recommendations to Mercy appropriate to the
case. Time after time, nowadays, they bring in the
distressing verdict of *Guilty but Insane*."

"It is a verdict which we ourselves use increasingly
in our own courts," I said.

"I am aware of that. No doubt the analogy will help
you to understand why many of us feel that the Insan-
ity verdict is being overworked."

"There are genuine cases of diminished responsibility before our courts," I said.

"And before ours too. I'm afraid we now receive defendants in large numbers who have been trained in irrationality from childhood by their parents and teachers, and by the influence of their environment. But we have always allowed for variations in personal responsibility by our official Recommendations to Mercy, which take all extenuating circumstances into account."

There was silence between us for some time after this. Evening descended upon us as we sped through the fields, and the summer sun was now low enough to beat through the carriage windows on to our faces. I began to feel drowsy. There was a calmness about the countryside and the little village stations through which we passed, a calmness due in part to the fact that it was Sunday. Stations were deserted. Occasionally we saw little groups of people in their Sunday best walking or talking in the village streets. At one point we saw a church emptying itself of its villagers after Evensong.

"That is a good thing to see," said Lamiel.

I thought this rather a sentimental utterance. It had an embarrassing quality, foreign—I thought—to the clear-minded, plain-spoken Lamiel. I decided to take him up on it.

"Can we really decide whether it is a good thing, when we don't know what those people are thinking or feeling?" I asked.

"We can indeed," Lamiel replied.

"But suppose they go to church only because they think it is the proper thing to do?"

"What better reason is there for going to church?

Would you have them go on the grounds that it is an improper thing to do?"

Lamiel pressed his question firmly, and I began to feel uncomfortable. As often in similar circumstances, the case which had seemed so obvious when I first took it up, began to seem elusive and weak when it was keenly challenged.

"Come along," said Lamiel. "What is your complaint against them?"

"Well," I said, "for all we know, they may have sat through a church service, paying very little attention to what they said or to what was said to them."

"Knowing human beings," said Lamiel, "I should think that almost certain to be the case."

"Then isn't it very hypocritical?"

"Nonsense," said Lamiel. "It is merely *human*, in a jusitifiable sense of that much-abused word. They are mostly simple villagers. They certainly cannot live at a feverish level of intellectual concentration or spiritual activity for more than a few moments at a time. They must necessarily go through a great deal of unanalysed repetition in the course of public worship. Does that detract from the value of their worship?"

"Their hearts ought to be in it..." I began, but Lamiel interrupted me.

"Their hearts are most certainly in it, or they wouldn't be there. They'd be in a pub instead. Let me ask you a question. Suppose your son comes into your room in the evening before he goes to bed. And suppose he says, 'Good night, father.' Would you stop him, and rebuke him, asking, 'My boy. Did you really mean that? Was your heart in it?' Of course not. His heart is in it, for he does it. He does it because he knows it is the proper thing to do. Those two sentences are merely two different ways of saying the same thing. If you expect his heart to be in it in the sense that he weighs reflectively every word he says—well, you are a fool. Human utterance isn't like that. God knows it isn't—even if you don't."

I felt rebuked, and tried to make amends.

"So," I said, "all the talk about the hypocrisy of worship which is just mechanical repetition, as they say, is..."

"Claptrap," said Lamiel, "Utter claptrap. *Good morning, Good evening, How are you?* are mechanical repetitions in that sense. Does that mean that you would be a better, more genuine man, if you never indulged in these courteous greetings. Of course not. The idea is nonsensical. I will tell you something else—the sort of thing your psychologists would tell you, if they knew any psychology. By saying *How are you?* you make yourself concerned about your friend's well-being. You have read von Hügel, I believe. Perhaps you remember this: 'I kiss my son not only because I love him, but in order that I may love him.' In the same way, men go to church not only because they wish to worship God, but in order that they may wish to worship God."

"Then the mere act of going to church, however desultory the intention, however ill-considered the motive, is sufficient..." I ventured.

"Not sufficient, but the main thing. For it is the act of obedience which is the root of all worship and of all faith. And, of course, it is infinitely better than staying at home on earnest conscientious grounds. Human beings have this limitation, that they learn to pray by praying, they learn to worship by worshipping. So that obedience to external precept is always necessary

at the start. Otherwise there never is a start. Love itself is nourished from obedience. And a pretty severe
discipline of obedience is requisite for any man, before
he recognises in himself anything that he dare call love
for God."

"Of that I can't speak..." I began.

"Then don't," said Lamiel, "until you can."

After that, of course, I didn't. I held my peace for
the rest of the journey, and reflected upon the possible
discomforts, so soon to be realised, of having an angel
about the house.

The Angel in the House

It is not much fun to live the spiritual life with the spiritual equipment of an artist.

THOMAS MERTON: *The Sign of Jonas*

At first things went quite smoothly at home. I was able to explain to my wife who Lamiel was and what he was doing, and she was relieved that he had no special designs upon the family. The children asked Lamiel childish questions, but he gave them good answers and therefore got on famously with them. I introduced him as "Uncle Lamiel," of course. The absence of a surname made this the only thing to do. Thomas, my eldest boy, remarked that I had never previously referred to an Uncle Lamiel, but I explained that he was an uncle by courtesy, not by family relationship. Younger members of the family eyed him critically at this juncture, and it was even openly observed that Uncle Lamiel had not hitherto distinguished himself at birthday-times by the despatch either of greeting cards or of postal orders. Lamiel accepted this criticism quite ruefully and gave a frank account of himself.

"I would send you cards if I could," he said, "but I live a very long way off; and indeed where I come from there are no post offices at all."

Although this admission created a somewhat modest estimate of Lamiel's home environment in the minds of the young, it was also taken in very good faith as evidence of the new uncle's good intentions. It was inevitable that Lamiel should get on well with children, because he liked to be questioned. Besides he told them stories—and very good stories they were too, all about dwarfs and goblins, dragons and buried treasure. He had the knack of talking about these things without that apologetic touch which nowadays ruins so much of our story-telling to children. I remarked on this to him after the children had left us to go to bed.

"Nourishment for the imagination," he said. "They need it. Desperately they need it in this mechanical age. The whole natural world should be alive with good and evil creatures in children's stories. Yet even here you have reached a new level of debasement to the subnatural. What can you do with a civilisation which nurtures its children on tales that attempt to give faces and personalities to buses and railway trains?"

He sighed reflectively and leaned back in his armchair. It promised to be a homely evening. Lamiel was at his gentlest after his hour with the children. He was appreciatively trying his first glass of beer; and we were both glad of the quiet after our long journey. Unfortunately, however, our peace was disturbed. Julian Farrago called to see us, and I had to resign myself to an evening of stirring talk.

I had known Julian for many years. We had a common interest in writing. Julian had published short stories and poems. The reviewers found the former "too slight" and the latter "too indisciplined"; and I suppose they were right, for Julian was cursed with a range of talents and a diversity of interests which unfitted him for success in an age of specialisation. For he also painted pictures—water colours which occasionally sold to London stores, and oil paintings which never sold to anyone. Moreover, he was a musician too. He played the flute and composed. I think he gave more time to this than he did either to his writing or to his painting. Nor was he content to fashion little trios for flute, violin and piano: he also wrote elaborate fully-scored cantatas to words by outlandish poets. This wide range of his talents and interests probably prevented him from achieving distinction in any one direction. He regarded himself as a painter, gave most of his attention to music, and was in practice most successful as a writer.

Julian was unmarried. He ran a bachelor establishment on rather ostentatiously bohemian lines. That is to say, he rarely went to bed before 3 A.M. and never got up before 11; he ate all his meals from a tray, seated, legs up, on a settee; and he never put things away. He lived on a small annuity supplemented by occasional profits from sale of work.

"I just had to come out," he said, accepting a glass of beer and settling down. "I worked all night on a picture, and then compensated by an afternoon nap. I tired myself; but it was worth it. I'm really getting somewhere."

"What are you painting?" asked Lamiel, obviously trying to be courteous.

"What am I painting!" Julian laughed aloud. "What am I painting! Good God, I'm painting a picture of course. Not a bunch of highland cattle standing in a pool, if that's what you mean."

"I thought it was a simple question," said Lamiel. "I'm interested to hear what it is that you are representing on the canvas, that's all."

"This really is rather rich," said Julian. "I'm an artist, not a movie-director. Strictly speaking I'm not painting anything. It's an abstract. There is an idea behind it, of course: but no representationalism. Good God, no."

"Since there is an idea, let's hear it," I said, trying to bridge the gap between my two companions' modes of thought.

"*Idea* is too literal a word," said Julian. "There's no naturalistic theme: just a unity of images achieved by the rhythm of the composition. Dominating the picture-space is a white tennis ball, poised centrally against a very solid-looking brick wall. This is the fantasy-element of the composition, and I've made it the focal point of a functional trigonometrical pattern. Surrounding it, there's a recessional grouping of linear elements, giving the positional context of the ball in relation to the ground level, the top of the wall and the eye of an off-stage spectator. The charm of the picture lies in the blend of unsophisticated childishness and scientific pretension. There's a naughty dig at the photographers too. The thing is so laughably static."

"What will viewers make of it?" asked Lamiel.

"Nothing at all, I expect. But what does that matter?"

"I imagine," said Lamiel, "that the prime end of painting a picture is to provide something significant to look at."

Julian turned to me in horror.

"I say, where on earth have you disinterred this relic of antiquity?" Then, seeing my embarrassment, he turned quickly to Lamiel. "You mustn't mind what I say. I daresay you're rich in old-world courtesy too; but I'm much too honest a man to practise that kind of thing. And I've no respect at all for the cloth."

"I realise that," said Lamiel quietly, "but if you have any respect for art, there is at least some common ground between us, and we can make shift to communicate. I just wondered what you considered the main purpose of artistic creation to be."

"Self-expression," said Julian. "Whether it's literature, painting or music, self-expression is the only thing that matters. This abstract, for instance; I just had to bring it out of me. It's been there since childhood; since I first threw a ball against a wall with the hope that perhaps it wouldn't fall to earth. The emotional pattern was there inside me, crying out to be released, either on paper or on canvas. And obviously canvas was the right medium for it. All that matters for an artist is that he should give sincere expression to the emotional patterns inside him. He mustn't distort them. He must be absolutely honest, and not overlay them with artifice or swamp them with the respectable conventions of crude representationalism. It takes courage; but it's got to be done."

"One moment," said Lamiel. "Whence do these emotional patterns derive?"

"From the roots of a man's being," said Julian. "They are the stuff of his soul."

"Ah, you believe in the soul?"

"Not in an airy-fairy spiritual nothing that goes winging off to heaven when the heart is snuffed out."

"What sort of a thing is your soul, then?"

"Why, it's the flame of all my vitality. The thing that makes me glow when I hear a symphony; the thing that lights up when I fall in love."

"It sounds like the good old appetites to me—the desire of the senses and the lust of the flesh."

"Exactly," said Julian. "You could learn our language easily, if you really tried. Can't you see that what you call lust and appetite—the vital urge to taste and feel and drink and love—can't you see that *that* is what we call soul?"

"I can see perfectly," said Lamiel, "and of course it explains everything. Your self-expression is mere sensual indulgence. And that is why your philosophy of art requires no theory of communication."

"Of course it doesn't. An artist seeks to body forth his soul, as someone put it. What more sincere labour than to utter spontaneously that basic urge to live fully and richly?"

"Let me ask you a question," said Lamiel. "When you have completed a picture or a poem, do you say—'Thank God, I've got that out of my system!' or—'Yes; at last; that's what I felt; that's what I meant. Now I know'?"

"The latter, of course," said Julian.

"Good. Now we can make headway. What you have just admitted proves that, when you create in art, you do not merely express something which already exists inside you: rather you organise something which was previously disorganised—or discover something which was previously hidden."

"Yes, I'll grant you that."

"Very well then. This *you* which organises cannot be the same thing as the material which it organises."

"I suppose not."

"And since the material to be organised is the content or residue of your emotional experience, the organiser is presumably something other. What is he?"

"I cannot answer that."

"No, because your philosophy precludes the possibility of answering it. The organiser is the creative impulse. And we have proved that the creative impulse is not the same thing as the emotional content within you, but is something which uses and organises that content. Whence, I ask, is this impulse? Old-fashioned people might have called it a spiritual gift. But you have whittled away man's spirituality in a morass of appetite and desire. You cannot answer my question, for the simple reason that you have no religion."

Lamiel spoke without anger, but Julian responded as though he had been slapped in the face.

"No religion! I resent that as a shameful and unjustifiable insult. I am proud to admit that I have no use for what you parsons would call religion—for archaic and moribund institutionalism, drab mechanical liturgies, and all the morbid nonsense of perfectly healthy people pretending to be miserable sinners—when their chief sin is the lie of pretending to be wicked. I hate the hypocrisy of it with all my soul. But I'm a deeply religious man—every artist is; so religious that I've no use for the hollow mockery of your artificial ceremonies, empty observances and petty morality. My art is my religion. No priest ever served his God more faithfully than I serve my art."

"But if your art is self-expression, devoted service to your art is merely self-service."

This was a shrewd blow, for it made quite clear that Julian's case wouldn't hold water. I was impressed by the ingenuity of Lamiel's logic, and by the cool way in which he planted his fatal shot. But I was also apprehensive about how Julian would respond. Could he take it? Could he say straightforwardly—'You've beaten me there. I shall have to drop that line'? Or would he be too weak to admit his own weakness?

Would he try to wriggle out—into irrelevance or abuse? I watched him intently to see which line he would take. I saw how he mentally appreciated an honest dialectical defeat and trembled on the edge of openly admitting it. But something got the better of candour, some long-ingrained habit of self-indulgence, perhaps; some undisciplined constitutional assertiveness; and, with a bang, he came down on the side of red-faced bluster.

"Who are you," he cried, "to speak of selfishness to a man who has devoted himself, body and soul, to his high calling—sacrificing food, sleep, comfort, and friendship to the enrichment of life by the creation of beauty?"

"Really," said Lamiel calmly, "really you can't have it both ways. You spoke a moment ago of a life devoted to self-expression. Now you speak of a life devoted to the creation of beauty—a quite different and, in my view, altogether more laudable pursuit. But if art is primarily the creation of beautiful things, then it is not primarily self-expression; so your former definition is proved invalid. Again, you now speak of your work as a *calling*. A little logic will make clear to you that there cannot be a call without a caller. If you are called to paint, presumably someone or something calls you. This is exactly the point I was trying to arrive at. You have led me there more quickly yourself. Who has called you? For this is really the same question I asked before. What is the source of the creative impulse by which alone you are enabled to work as an artist?"

Dialectically he had tied Julian up in knots. Julian knew this well enough. He got redder and redder, ruder and ruder, and all the more incoherent for being conscious that he was making a fool of himself.

"You are trying to drag your blasted religion in again. It was beaten off on the frontal approach, so you attempt to worm it in round the back. But you haven't answered *my* question. Who are you to talk like that to an artist who has striven and suffered as only artists can? You come from a world of dead artificialities and unnatural suburbanism to sermonise a man whose passion for art keeps him hard at work till four in the morning, with nothing but a coffee and a cigarette for sustenance!"

"Weigh your thoughts more carefully," said Lamiel, "instead of descending to abuse and self-display. Which is the more natural and the less artificial—to retire to bed with the coming of darkness and to rise with the dawn, or to work through the night with the civilised aids of electric lighting, hot drinks and tobacco? And as for religion, we must leave that out of the discussion, since we have agreed that the word carries widely different connotations for the two of us."

"It does indeed," Julian snarled. "For me it is a word to describe sacred things—love, work, feeling, beauty. For you it is all mixed up with puritanical taboos, snotty-nosed choirboys and rows of sex-starved spinsters, who have never learned to feel, let alone to pray. My whole life is a prayer. Every picture I paint is a prayer. In the only sacred sense of the word; the sense in which a Chinese vase or a Beethoven quartet is a prayer."

"You will pardon me for pointing out that the one is a piece of pottery, the other a piece of music."

Julian rose from his seat, trembling and flushed.

"I shall not pardon you at all. I shall leave your company for a purer atmosphere. You can swill your beer till midnight. *I* go back to my work."

He turned, stamped across the room, slammed the door, and was gone.

It was some moments before we allowed the silence to subside into conversation again. When I did speak, I was made to regret it.

"Rather a theatrical exit," I said. "Altogether too stagey for the self-forgetful servant of Art."

"That is ill-said," Lamiel replied in a tone of displeasure. "You kept pretty quiet during our discussion. Have the grace to refrain from personal criticism of your friend now that he is gone."

"I'm sorry," I said, "but you made it so plain that he is wrong."

"I may have done that. But I did not make it plain that he is wicked, as your statement uncharitably implies. I attacked his ideas, because they are bad ideas. But he does not live down to them. He works hard, and values what he creates for its own sake. He does not realise this; but he may one day come to think as soundly as he acts."

I was comforted by this; for I was beginning to feel that the friendship of one so sorely assaulted by Lamiel's dialectic cast something of a slur upon me.

"The philosophy of self-expression," Lamiel went on, after a pause, "is bad. It cannot exist alongside rational Christianity. For the Faith teaches that man is rooted in the Supernatural, and derives thence all the impulses, values and insights by which he is able to transfigure the life of the senses and of the mind. But the philosophy and cult of self-expression imply that there is in natural man a source of sacred illumination and a principle of beneficent growth which are suffic-

ient in themselves to spiritualise human existence. As I
said before, you cannot have it both ways. The creative impulse of the artist derives either from a supernatural or from a natural source. It is either given
from above—or it grows from below, rooted in man's
animality. If it grows from below, it is no more sacred
than any other physical impulse or appetite, and cannot possibly be exalted as a principle which com-
mands service and imposes obligations. Farrago treats
it, in practise, as a God-given impulse, requiring self-
dedication. In theory he professes the current doctrine
of aesthetic Naturalism. The two are irreconcilable.
Therefore he talks incoherent nonsense. But he is better than his talk....And therefore it might be a good
idea if you were to slip along and have a friendly chat
with him, before going to bed. I shall retire now.
Good night."

Encounter by Night

What can this work be? Sure, you will say, it must be
an allegory; or (as the writer calls it) a religious PARA-
BLE, showing the dreadful danger of self-righteousness?
I cannot tell. Attend to the sequel.

JAMES HOGG: *Confessions of a Justified Sinner*

Left alone, I decided to follow Lamiel's advice—or
rather his instructions. Julian's house was but half a
mile away, and he would certainly not have gone
straight to bed. So I stepped out into the darkness and
swung my way jauntily down the street, feeling rather
pleased with myself. I had not helped to provoke the
altercation, and my role was that of the benevolent
peacemaker. I could afford to be magnanimous. Sentences full of large-hearted tolerance and forbearance
shaped themselves in my head as I strode towards the
pacific interview and considered how I should begin—"You're a bit mixed up in your ideas, Julian, old
boy, but you've a heart of gold....Philosophising just
isn't in your line, old chap: stick to your work and
don't fret yourself over aesthetic theory....Nonsense,
my dear fellow, you talked utter nonsense—I say, is
that the new painting? You've certainly got something
there!"

It occurred to me, as I walked, that I had been
pretty unimpressive myself during the evening's conversation. Even Lamiel had remarked on my failure to
contribute anything. There might be an opportunity

now to salvage a little dignity for myself before the day was quite done. Ought I not, perhaps, to speak as the impartial spectator—better still, as the judge—weighing the merits of the two cases he has listened to, superior to the prejudices of both, and able to pass judgment at the end? This line would have the advantage of giving a touch of posthumous significance and profundity to my rather weak silence amid the discussion. "I listened carefully to both of you, Julian. I wanted you both to have your say, and I was careful not to intervene. I'm sure you'd like to hear my summing-up." Yes, that was a very good word, *summing-up*. He would be forced to attend to that respectfully—so reasonable, conclusive and *hors de combat*. "Well, Julian, my friend, you weren't at your best. I admit that Lamiel's ingenious verbal analysis was a little quibbling and indeed bordered on the pedantic. But you just did not stick to the point. You were too excited and not a little abusive. I'm afraid judgment must go against you—with costs, Julian, with costs. How about a drink to settle the legal bill and make the judge a little more disposed to be sympathetic? And then you must show me some of your new work. I'm most interested to see how you progress."

My step was jauntier than ever, and I almost walked straight past Julian's gate, so taken up was I in my judicial role. I bounded up the steps and knocked loudly on the door. There was no reply, so I tried the handle. It was locked. I knocked again, clattering on the door with my walking-stick. But only silence succeeded. Slowly I gave up hope. And I turned back, down the steps and out of the gate, in a mood of resentment and irritation. Deprived of the opportunity to distribute

discreet pardons, admonitions and pats on the back, I
felt, quite irrationally, that some malice in Julian had
brought the evening to this unsatisfactory conclusion.
I began to suspect that he didn't deserve my beneficent intentions. In a mood of unworthy spite he had
run petulantly from the course of my overflowing
goodwill.

I faced about and looked up at the great windows of
the house, a late Victorian building, combining together in peculiar nineteenth-century fashion all the
practical and aesthetic disadvantages of excessive
height and excessive narrowness. Sure enough the
whole place was in darkness. From the attic window
my eyes drifted over the sky, now dismally over-
clouded—disappointingly so after the sunny evening.
Not a star was visible. The heavy atmosphere promised rain, perhaps thunder. August clouds have their
own peculiar drabness, laying a dead hand of depres-
sion over the holiday season.

There was nothing for it but to get back home to
bed. I took my hand from the gate, turned, and fixed
my eyes on the single gas-lamp half-way between
where I stood and the end of the terrace. Its light was
the more vivid because behind it, in the main road at
right angles to this terrace, a huge factory blocked out
with blackness the sombre grey of the sky. As I moved
towards it, a shape detached itself from the black
background, passed beneath the lamp and slid up to
me.

I say *slid*, because the word suggests something in
the manner of our first meeting which is otherwise in-
describable. For there was an odd, even eerie, incon-
gruity between the solid clarity of the black figure
outlined in the lamplight and the smooth, almost in-

sidious, ease with which it glided into my presence. I stiffened inwardly when he spoke to me.

"You were seeking Mr. Farrago?"

"To no avail," I said, with a shrug.

I was thinking hard; for I suspected that I knew the man. Not that the features told me so. But I felt that I had previously experienced his smooth erectness of bearing and the black penetration of his eyes.

"I am staying with him."

There was nothing odd about this. Occasional visitors turned up and planted themselves upon Julian for a few days at a time. Still, it occurred to me that this tall, unbending, white-faced person was not of the usual pattern of Julian's artistic guests. Perhaps the face wouldn't look so white under a different sky. Certainly the complexion could ill afford the proximity of those uncompromisingly black points in the eye-sockets.

I passed no comment, and he spoke again.

"You think you know me, Mr.—"

He called me by my name. I started, and then remembered to smile.

"I still can't place you," I said.

"No, no...of course not. It is not to be expected."

"I presume you are an artist, yet your appearance..."

"Oh, please, please," he said, and raised his hand in a gesture of deprecation.

At once I understood. Lamiel's gesture. Lamiel's erectness. Lamiel's dark eyes.

"You have come with Lamiel..." I blurted.

He drew himself suddenly together.

"Not exactly. No, I have not come *with* Lamiel."

"But you are another..."

"Yes," he interrupted. "I too have come from above. But Lamiel does not know; and I shall be obliged if you will not tell him."

"I can't tell him," I laughed. "I don't know who you are."

"I'm sorry," he said. "Coffer is the name. I will not embarrass you with the official title. We have our little reservations. We have our gradations too. And it is not always advisable that the...er...lower hierarchical grades should know exactly what their superiors are about. That is why I ask you not to speak of me to Lamiel."

Not surprisingly, I drew in my breath with some awe at this indication of the speaker's exalted status. Then I began to wonder at his promptness in revealing it. In a man it would not have been good taste. But I was accustomed to Lamiel's forthrightness, and Coffer's openness seemed to be of a piece with it.

"I think I can trust your discretion," he went on.

"Of course," I said.

"Good. You have already realised, no doubt, that Lamiel is but a Guardian, acting under orders?"

"Yes." Lamiel had made it abundantly clear that his role was one of obedience.

"Perhaps too you have sensed that quality in him which fits him peculiarly for subordination. I will not call it a deficiency; for humility is a glorious virtue, glorious indeed. And its exercise, I may add, brings peace and joy. But some of us are called to shoulder responsibility—and there is sometimes little peace or joy in that. The role of authority imposes its penalties: but they must be endured. We suffer: I do not deny it: and suffering is something which the obedient Guardians will never fully understand."

Of course I realised that Heaven couldn't be entirely populated by creatures under orders. And I looked with new respect upon the pale complexion and the shadowed eye-sockets, the high furrowed forehead, and the drooping corners of the thin mouth. The muscles beneath the prominent cheek-bones twitched, and the eyes narrowed, as if in all the concentration of grief. Then he suddenly flung back his head and touched me on the shoulder.

"This is not the time for the self-indulgence of misery. There is work to be done. I have appraised your good sense and discernment, and I shall put absolute confidence in you accordingly. You must understand that I have responsibilities in relation to Lamiel's visit here; responsibilities which I would gladly forgo. I wish it were permitted to me to speak with him face to face, as I speak to you. There would then be no cause to enlist your support in the surveillance of his performance. But we must learn to accept the higher role as patiently, if not as joyfully, as the Guardian accepts his role of obedient service. Nevertheless, I regret the necessity to share the burden of authority. It is hard."

Again he drew tight his frame, his lips, his jaws, and narrowed his tormented eyes.

"I believe," he said slowly, "that you are one who would not shirk a task, even though it were burdened with the responsibilities of authoritative and decisive action."

His words confused me. In my bewilderment I could see nothing clearly except that something unpleasant was going to be demanded of me. Obsessed with curiosity as to what it might be, I trembled nervously in the ensuing silence, while he slowly turned his head towards me and looked me up and down, as though measuring my capacities. Gradually his features relaxed into a smile, and he nodded confidently.

"It will be all right," he said. "Certainly it will be all right, I can see that you are the man we need. ...Tell me, why do you think Lamiel is here?"

"He told me that he is here to observe."

"No doubt he told you so. But what do *you* think is the reason for his visit?"

"Naturally I accepted his word."

"Of course, of course. It was a true one. Certainly he *thinks* he is here to observe. We purposely gave him that impression. But I should like you to understand what is behind it all. He thinks he is here to observe: but in fact he is here to *be* observed."

"You mean it is some kind of test?"

"Exactly. It would not do for the Guardians to realise it; but they are being tested. As a result of their performance in this test, some of them will be promoted to offices of higher significance; others, I regret to say, will be demoted to even humbler work. It's a question of measuring their capacity for shouldering greater responsibility. Above all, we must gauge their independence, resourcefulness and capacity to initiate. Lamiel is a friend of yours; but friendship must not destroy candour. I believe you might yourself question the likelihood of his winning promotion on these grounds. I mean, his very virtues dispose him especially to subordination. There is a tendency to avoid taking the initiative, perhaps—a fondness for the role of the commanded?"

I could not deny that these words chimed in with thoughts that had fitfully occurred to me; though I had suppressed them as the products of misunderstanding. Now I was not so sure.

"I should agree," I said, "that he overstresses sometimes the fact that he is under orders. And he is very
dogmatic in argument."

"Precisely. The textbook mentality. You have already found him too narrow in his ideas, too superfi-
cial—too literal—in his judgments."

I recollected what Lamiel had said in the train
about the church-goers. He had put me right—or so it
had seemed at the time. I wondered whether perhaps
I had been right after all, and I nodded in sympathy
with Coffer's criticism.

"I do not want to distress you," Coffer went on,
"but Lamiel will probably have to be declared more
fit for obedience than for leadership. It may even be
the case that, far from being promoted, he must be
considered as a candidate for possible demotion."

This seemed to carry the argument much further
than I myself had intended—and than my words had
warranted—and I hastened to retract.

"Oh, no, I should be sorry to think that."

"We should all be sorry. Yet it might nevertheless be
our painful duty to speak the painful truth. A weak
servant can do great damage in our work, even in a
comparatively humble role. It is essential that the
right person should be in the right job. That is why I
am inviting you to assist me in this responsible work of
assessing his capacities. I wish you to observe him
critically. You must judge him impartially and not allow feeling or sentiment to bias you in his favour or
prejudice you against him. You too must be prepared
to suffer... and there is no suffering like that of speaking the painful truth in judgment of the weak."

He drew back his neck stiffly and strained his eyes
sadly into the blackness.

"Has Lamiel had cause yet to speak to my friend Farrago?"

"Yes," I said. "The interview was not a very happy one."

"Ah, you have seen some failing of sympathy, some narrowness of vision, some blindness to the artistic stature of my friend?"

I recollected Lamiel's strictures. Certainly they represented a highly intellectualised triumph over Julian. But they had satisifed me at the time. And now I didn't quite know how to express the feeling that my companion, though thinking on the right lines, was doing so with quite unjustified exaggeration.

"There was probably too much quibbling and pedantry in his treatment of Julian," I admitted, "but I don't think it did any harm."

Coffer raised his eyes and drew in a deep slow breath.

"There are occasions for intellectual argument," he said, "and there are occasions for restraint and awe before the sacredness of creative integrity. Farrago is an artist, and the artist is not as other men. He cannot be docketed in any system of rigid classification. There is a fine spirituality in Farrago—a flaming, lawless spirituality which utterly transcends anything that the mere literalist and dogmatist can comprehend. The artist is our especial care above. And Farrago is my chosen protégé, unschooled as yet, perhaps, but dead right in his soul. We must be humble before the artist, for he endures much—suffers much in the pursuit of fulfilment for his inviolable inner integrity. In that pursuit he suffers ridicule and blame, the scorn of society and the taunts of the respectable. And worse things too he suffers: for he *must* originate, he *must* explore, even if it involves sin and self-abuse, the sacrifice of friendship and of health. We cannot apply to him the canons of our systematised morality: for he makes of nameless sins a martyrdom in the cause of self-discovery. The true artist ascetically forsakes the security of morality as the hermit forsakes the ways of comfort. The artist, self-fulfilled in passion, is the prophet of the unashamedly incarnate soul. On the altar of self-realisation he offers up a torn and bruised morality. Is he not a saviour of his fellows? He is: he is with the saints."

Carried away by these tremendous words, he paused for a moment in an infectious agony of awe, and then silently lowered his head as though in tranquil prayer. Something of the sacredness of his convictions stirred me, and I too began to frame a silent petition; but immediately he pulled himself together, put his hand on my shoulder and gently jerked me out of my intention.

"This is not the time for meditation," he said. "Before we part, I must make quite sure that you understand your commission. You will observe Lamiel with a clear, though not unfriendly, eye; and you will be especially alert to notice whether he seems to manifest those qualities most necessary for creatures who are called to lead, to direct and to initiate. Is there too much dogmatic literalism in his teaching? Is he too doctrinaire, too much a victim of blind, unreflecting obedience? Does he lack tact or sympathy in dealing with others? You are an educationist. You are accustomed to the work of weighing people up and assessing their qualities. Indeed you are peculiarly fitted for giving us assistance in this work. I shall need all the information you can give me, when next we meet. Now go home; and get a good night's sleep."

He turned abruptly, ran up the steps of Julian's door and let himself in with a key.

As I walked home I was troubled. From the first I had found Lamiel an amiable and good-tempered being; and I had honestly admired his clarity of thought and utterance as the marks of his authoritative angelic status. When he made statements which sounded, on first hearing, too dogmatic or even bigoted, I had found that they did not in the long run alter my opinion of him as a fair-minded critic of human affairs. Rather they altered my view of dogmatism and bigotry. Indeed he had seemed to correct my view of these things. Now, of couse, I had the highest authority for believing that I had been misled. Yet though it have been easy, at the time, to sympathise with Coffer's criticisms of Lamiel, it was by no means easy to adjust myself permanently to this new point of view. For one thing, Lamiel had been hard on Julian's views, but he had certainly not been hard on Julian. Again, although Lamiel had frequently hurt me by sudden rebukes and denials, the hurt had always, on reflection, seemed worthwhile for the intellectual or moral clarification it had accompanied.

I saw that is was going to be an arduous, even painful, task to measure just where and when Lamiel overstepped the mark so as to fail in tolerance, understanding or independence. Coffer's remarks about suffering came home to me with a new intensity. As the image of his tortured eyes recurred to me, I braced myself tensely and quickened my step.

The Guardian Observed

Agnosticism is going, going, gone. Not it, but Pantheism is now, and will long be, the danger of Religion.

BARON VON HÜGEL

Next day we breakfasted early, and Lamiel suggested that a morning walk in the country might
freshen us up after our day of travelling. So it was
that, by ten o'clock, we were striding on to the downs
on the edge of the city, both of us rather quiet and
thoughtful. I was myself a little disappointed at the
prospect of the walk alone with Lamiel. I realised
that, if I were to sum him up properly, I should have
to see him and hear him in conversation with a third
party. I wanted to take note of his behaviour in con-
texts from which it was possible to detach myself, as
an observer. I was therefore highly delighted when I
caught sight of a familiar figure treading the path
ahead of us. It was my friend and colleague Lloyd Ol-
lerton, a man whose whole philosophy of life was
bound to clash with Lamiel's and whose utterances
would certainly make this clear. Lloyd, a wiry, tousle-
headed little man, was wearing walking shorts and
carrying a rucksack. Plainly he was off for a solitary
walking tour, a practice to which he was much ad-
dicted.

"You must have a talk with him," I said to Lamiel.
"He will argue, and you'll enjoy it."

"I believe you really mean that *you'll* enjoy it." That

was all Lamiel said in reply.

Lloyd, when we overtook him, came fully up to expectations. He surveyed our full-suited urban appearance with something of disdain. He seemed anxious from the start to make clear that he was taking country walking seriously, and that our casual escape from the city did not put us on a level with him. Eager to stoke up this mood and to provoke an argument, I tried the force of irony.

"If your primus is reasonably accessible, Lloyd," I said, "perhaps you could treat us to morning coffee before our ways part."

"It's a luxury I'm happy to dispense with on these occasions," he remarked dryly. "I think my idea of a holiday is not quite the same as yours."

"You are running away from civilisation for a day or two," said Lamiel. "Not a bad idea at all."

"I run away from it whenever I can," said Lloyd. "It corrupts the soul."

"And Nature provides you with spiritual refreshment," I said, hopeful of controversy.

"She does indeed—when she is approached in the proper way; and that means in solitude."

Lloyd emphasised the last words significantly; and Lamiel took the hint.

"We shall not be with you for long," he said.

"Lamiel here is in orders, as you can see," I said. "He would not encourage you to rely upon Nature for your soul's nourishment."

"I am not concerned with what he would encourage," said Lloyd. "He has his professional job to do; and no doubt he does it well. For myself, I know that the nearer one is to Nature, the nearer one is to God."

The ball was rolling now. I knew that Lamiel wouldn't be able to resist this.

"I think you *mean* rightly there," he said, "but your statement won't do. The cannibal is nearer to Nature than the poor slum widow who wears her fingers to the bone trying to bring up her children decently. Would she be any nearer to God if you transported her to a cottage in the hills?"

"Other things being equal, she would."

Lamiel mused a little.

"Yes, perhaps you are right. Other things being equal. But isn't it the other things which chiefly determine her nearness to God? In the city she is further from Nature than the savage cannibal. Yet surely even there she is nearer to God than he."

"We can't say," said Lloyd, "for we haven't yet decided whether the cannibal is a God-fearing man who boils his fellow-creatures for *bona fide* religious purposes and devours them on conscientious grounds, or whether he titivates his perverse appetite without regard to moral scruples."

"You have given your case away," said Lamiel. "You have admitted that nearness to God is not dependent upon proximity to Nature, but on obedience to some kind of moral code."

"When I say that Nature brings a man nearer to God, I am assuming in man a certain moral integrity."

"Which makes the approach to God possible," said Lamiel. "A rash assumption. But it shows that you don't regard Nature as the prime vehicle of salvation."

"You're arguing in a circle," I said.

"In a spiral," said Lamiel, "which is the best way to argue."

"Wait a minute," said Lloyd. "This word *salvation*:

I can't accept it, as you use it; so your criticism breaks down. I don't believe in a moralistic God, who's got His head so stuffed up with notions of propriety that He can take notice of nothing but acts of petty thieving and trivial dishonesty. My God is much bigger than that. He's not just a glorified magistrate, forever judging, forever indulging Himself in stern condemnations or magnanimous grants of pardon. He's a source of growth, not a personified bunch of taboos and inhibitions. If you want to meet Him, come up into the hills at dawn—and come alone. You don't need to ask questions about Him then. You just feel Him."

"Round and round," said Lamiel. "I'm not sure that *circle* wasn't the right word, after all. Why can't you have a God who is bigger still? Not only the Creator of the dawn, but also a Redeemer, personally interested in how you and I behave? Moreover, your argument is not consistent. You have already admitted that moral integrity is a human prerequisite for experience of God through contact with Nature. Why is this so? If God is not interested in morality, why is He so extraordinarily whimsical—and, I may add, so oddly inconsistent—as to deny to the reprobate the vision which He grants to the upright?"

"It isn't a question of God's interest, but of man's capacity," said Lloyd. "It takes a pure-minded man to sense God in the hills. There's nothing mysterious about that. It's a law of Nature."

"But why should Nature prefer the good man to the bad man?" asked Lamiel. "Can't you see what you're doing? You're anxious to keep a God of Nature who is merely felt by man. But you keep dragging into your scheme of things a code of morality which naturalism cannot supply or substantiate."

"Morality is one thing and religion is another. Morality is a social arrangement. Religion is an emotional experience."

"Is it a good experience or a bad one?"

"A good one, of course."

"What principle in your social morality makes it so?"

"It is good, in itself."

"Ah, then you have values independent of your social arrangements?"

"Certainly. The principles of growth and nourishment, which Nature pre-eminently manifests. It is by these that she is enabled to refresh us."

"Physically?"

"And spiritually."

"I give up," said Lamiel, and then, after a few moments of silence, added. "No. Answer me this question. Your God is not a God of morality, you say. Morality is a convenient earthly arrangment?"

"Yes," Lloyd agreed.

"But He is a principle of growth and nourishment, pre-eminently manifested in Nature's beauty and abundance?"

"True."

"Very well, then. Which does your God prefer—the virile, tough, handsome, well-built, healthy exploiter of the poor, or the ailing, feeble, undernourished creature who lives in the service of others?"

Lloyd hesitated a moment, and then said: "Frankly, He hasn't got preferences about that kind of thing."

"Ah!" Lamiel pounced on to this. "And is it a good thing or a bad thing to prefer the one to the other?"

"From our point of view, a good thing: I grant you that."

"Very well, from our point of view (which is the

only point of view we can possibly adopt) your God is inferior to us in lacking the capacity to respond to experience as it is good to respond. Why worship Him, why seek Him, if He is thus inferior to your fellow human beings? Surely the wise man will always seek the company of the superior and not the inferior being? You are self-condemned for going in search of a sub-human divinity. You would be more profitably occupied with fellow human beings back in the city; for they are better persons than your God."

"But they can't provide that spiritual refreshment of which we have spoken."

"*Spiritual* is the wrong word. You have admitted your God less than human. He does not therefore deserve the title *God;* for it is a linguistic fact that the word refers to a being more exalted than man. The refreshment you get from Nature is mere physical refreshment, thoroughly wholesome and thoroughly worth seeking. But be so logical as to refrain from mixing God up in the business."

"I have met your kind before," said Lloyd, quite unperturbed. "You have your own vocabulary and your own set of concepts, and you try to make everybody else use them in your own limited way."

"You have a right to describe the laws of logic as a limitation; but it is a limitation which only the irrational can eschew."

"Why pursue me with these reproaches? Why not leave me to my happiness here on the downs—and return to your own happiness among the buses and lorries, the smoke and the machinery?"

"You know well enough," said Lamiel, "that I prefer the country to the city as you do—and, oddly enough, for the same reason. Because the Hand of

God is plainly before us here, and not so in the material environment of the city. But this God *is* God. And therefore greater and better than you or me. And therefore more sensitive to evil and suffering than you or me. And therefore a God of morality as well as of beauty and abundance. More than that; a God of Love. Not only to be sensed, but to be obeyed; not only obeyed, but loved. Think about it when next you feel Him. It may be that you know more than you think."

It was some moments after we parted from Lloyd that Lamiel turned to me with an abrupt question.

"Were you satisfied with my performance this time?"

"Oh, yes, yes," I said awkwardly.

"Full marks, then?"

I laughed nervously, uncertain what he was getting at, yet inwardly apprehensive of some dreadful discovery.

"You are thinking," he went on, "that I have perhaps improved since last night, in temper if not in argumentative ingenuity?"

"I always admire your skill in argument," I said.

"Good!"

He began to swing his arms more decisively as he walked, and for a few minutes he hummed audibly a tiresomely repetitive melody. I felt ill at ease, and was relieved when he suddenly jerked into conversation again.

"I'm going to ask you a question," he said.

"Fire away!" I replied, with a painfully forced casualness.

"This is it. How would you distinguish a true servant of God from a traitor?"

"I haven't the least idea," I said, relieved that Lamiel was not launched on a theoretical course, and apparently not disposed to plumb my private thoughts
more deeply.

"I thought not," he said. "So I will tell you one
thing which it is useful to remember in this connection. You should take especial notice how a person
speaks, not of other things, but of God. This will tell
you a lot."

"I suppose it must," I said.

"Of course," Lamiel added, "the case may be so elementary that this difficult question need not be
asked."

"What do you mean?"

"I mean that it may only be necessary to notice
whether the person in question ever does speak of God
at all. He will, if God is much in his mind. He may
not, if God is rarely in his mind—or if he wishes to exclude God from his thoughts."

"That is sound enough," I said.

"It is. Very sound. Full marks again, in fact?"

I managed a more convincing laugh this time. Lamiel turned to watch it. Rather too inquisitively, I
thought. Then he changed the subject again, so that I
was a little surprised; for it was not usual for him to
jump about in conversation from one topic to another.
On the contrary, he was in the habit of running every
subject to earth before he forsook it.

"By the way," he said, "you never told me what happened last night, when you went out to smooth things
over with Julian."

"I'm afraid he was not in. Very unusual, but there it
is."

"So you came back home?"

"Yes," I said, rather hesitantly, "I just came back."

"I see....You have read *Paradise Lost?*"

Again the quick change of subject. Lamiel's odd way of talking quite astonished me. I began to wonder whether something untoward had upset him and made him restless. Could he somehow have got wind of the fact that he was under observation, that he was involved in a test which could determine his future? I resolved to mark him even more closely. For I had learned from the psychologists that the loose talker, who hops from topic to topic, very often reveals himself plainly in his casual remarks.

"Yes," I said. "Of course I know *Paradise Lost.*"

"I sometimes wonder," said Lamiel, "whether Milton puts too much emphasis on the deception practised on man by the fallen angels. Does he, perhaps, put the thing on too intellectual a plane?"

"The case has been argued," I admitted. "But we must remember that, at the crucial point, Satan wins his way by an appeal to Eve's vanity."

"Yes," said Lamiel thoughtfully. "Yes, we must remember that."

And thus he dropped that subject too. Indeed I was wondering whether I should ever be able to sum him up. But one thing was clear. He was not revealing the kind of grasp and purposiveness which one seeks in a candidate for promotion, in any field. There was a lack of grip and a lack of direction about his conversation and his bearing towards me—a tentativeness and an apparent uncertainty which suggested that he was ill at ease. For the first time I began to feel that he needed help—that he needed me, not perhaps to guide him, but to steady him a little. I had been warned of this situation and prepared for it. I must accept the fact that it might even become my duty to check and restrain this disarming, yet oddly disquieted spirit.

When we got home, we met a visitor at the door, just on the point of leaving—the rector. A big, heavy man, with dark bushy eyebrows, thick-lensed spectacles and a short neck, the rector had at the best of times an overbearing appearance. His rather clipped staccato manner of speaking added to the general impression of formidableness. Actually, as so often in the case of big, cumbersome clerics, his exterior sharpness was but a protection for a tender-hearted benevolence.

"I've waited an hour for you," he said. "I've sacrificed a meeting, but I can't stay any longer."

I introduced Lamiel as "my friend Lamiel" and hoped for the best.

"C. of E.?" queried the rector, eyeing his clerical collar.

Lamiel laughed disarmingly. The rector tried to penetrate him.

"Roman?"

Again Lamiel laughed. The rector turned to me.

"I can making nothing of this. Is he one of us?"

"Oh, yes," I said, "he's one of us."

"That's all right," said the rector. "You can never tell with these cheerful-looking types."

The survey began again.

"Catholic or Evangelical?"

"Both," said Lamiel.

"Doesn't tell us much," said the rector. "Do you burn incense in your church?"

"Great clouds of it," said Lamiel.

"Umph," grunted the rector. "Not an extremist, I hope. You subscribe to the Thirty-Nine Articles."

"I can't make head or tail of them," said Lamiel.

"Well, that's honest. You're firm on Grace, I trust, as well as on the doctrine of the Church?"

"Firm as a rock."

"Umph." The rector grunted again. "One of these novel post-war mixtures, I'll be bound. You can't classify them. When it comes to the colour of their churchmanship, they hedge and smile, instead of answering a plain question plainly. Westcott House, I'll wager."

"No," said Lamiel. "I'm afraid you'd consider my theological training irregular, by your standards."

"Not at all surprised. I know what things are like these days. It's hard enough to get ordinands. But you've got a cultured background. I can see that."

"Thank you," said Lamiel.

"Smell it a mile off. One of the ancient universities, I presume?"

"Yes. Very ancient. The most ancient and venerable of all."

The rector roared with laughter and clapped Lamiel on the back.

"I knew it. I can always spot an Oxford man. We joke about it. But we're very proud at heart, seriously proud, not to have been brought up at the other place."

He pointed downwards with his finger, and grinned.

"I should think we are," said Lamiel.

"We should get on well together," said the rector.

"We must have a chat before you go. But I can't stay now. Awfully sorry. Good-bye."

And so we went inside, where I was surprised to find a telegram awaiting me. Lamiel eyed it with evident interest as my wife handed it to me. He seemed to be waiting for me to open it, as though he were concerned. This annoyed me slightly, so that I just stuffed it in my pocket unopened. Lamiel shrugged his shoulders without saying anything, and I left the room and went out into the garden. Alone, I opened the telegram.

MEET ME AT THE HONEYCROSS AT THREE
O'CLOCK URGENT STOP COFFER STOP

Frankly, I was not pleased. The thing was an order, and I resented it. Too many people were getting at me, I thought. I was becoming involved in machinations which were definitely not to my taste. The element of intrigue about this business was distasteful. Coffer's exalted rank among the angels and his injunctions about secrecy condemned me to a course of action involving pretence. For it was clear that I ought not to speak of my appointment either to Lamiel or to my wife. It would be wrong, I felt, to call this course dishonest, when it was recommended to me by an authority so unimpeachable. Or would it? I began to imagine the kind of comment Lamiel himself might make in reply to this conclusion. I was convinced that he would split the argument right open. But surely the incorrigible dogmatic certainty and that inflexible moral pedantry were the very things in Lamiel that had to be watched as possible dangers. Surely these were the very weaknesses which would probably produce for him a poor showing in the test. It was my business to rise above his dogmatism and moral pedantry, and to judge him as his superiors would judge him. I braced myself for my onerous and grievous role.

But in order to reduce the distasteful element of mystery in the business, I decided to try to contact Coffer on the phone, and I rang up Julian. He answered the phone and I remembered to begin the conversation with a few friendly overtures calculated to dispel any possible animosity left over from the talk of the previous night. Julian was quite amicable.

"You can't be held responsible for your guests' discourtesy," he said, "or for their stupidity either, for that matter. But try to keep better company, old man. I should hate you to be lost by the wayside."

"Don't worry about me," I said. "I'm glad you're not put out.... Oh, by the way, could I have a word with Coffer before I ring off?"

"With who?"

"Coffer."

"Never heard of him."

"Your visitor."

"I haven't got a visitor."

"Oh, come, I saw him enter your house last night."

"Then you were drunk or dreaming. I tell you, I'm alone, and have been for a fortnight."

"Oh," I said bewildered. "That's that then."

We rang off. And my first thoughts were of utter dismay. A conversation undertaken to clear up a mystery had but increased it fourfold. Coffer had spoken as though his relationship with Julian were as open and natural as my relationship with Lamiel. Could it be that he was living invisibly in Julian's house? The idea was absurd. Yet no other conclusion seemed possible. It appeared that Coffer was indulging in all those superfluous conjuring tricks which Lamiel and the other Guardians had been enjoined to eschew. This, in itself, put the relationship with Coffer on an altogether less pleasant plane than the relationship with Lamiel. I was tempted to think that there was something about this new relationship, not only unpleasant, but positively unhealthy. Indeed I was on the brink of what, a few minutes later, began to seem an astonishing outrage—of questioning Coffer's honesty and suspecting his credentials. A lucky thought saved me from pursuing this dangerous train of ideas. The explanation dawned upon me with laughable suddenness and clarity. Coffer had obviously enjoined Julian to secrecy, and my friend had quite properly refused to confide in me. Why should he confide in me? What evidence had I given of an established acquaintance with Coffer? What evidence could I give? Plainly the injunction to secrecy prevented my saying anything to Julian about Coffer's private commission to me.

Had I already put my foot in it by the mere mention of Coffer to Julian? Had I, by this act, betrayed the trust imposed in me? Still worse, had I rendered myself unfit for the discharge of the responsibilities hanging over me? I was thoroughly disquieted. Above all, I was apprehensive that perhaps an ignominious scolding lay ahead for me—a thorough dressing-down by Coffer, on the grounds that I was not discreet enough to keep quiet about something for twenty-four hours. I resolved to keep an absolutely unbroken guard upon my tongue until the afternoon meeting with Coffer.

And so firm was I in my resolution that I must have appeared taciturn, even morose, at the lunch table. Lamiel talked to my wife and to the children, whilst I sat in dogged silence. And I maintained this role as we reclined in deck-chairs in the garden for an hour or so after our meal. I thought that Lamiel had a nap. Certainly he too lapsed into silence. He said nothing of note until I rose to make specious apologies, ready to set out and keep my appointment. Then he indulged again in one of those oddly disconnected and irrelevant pieces of conversation which had marked our intercourse during the morning.

"One moment," he said, opening his eyes and staring straight at me. "I should like to try an old question on you."

"Well?" I asked, impatient to be off.

"Must we believe that a thing is good because God wills it, or that God wills a thing because it is good?"

"It's a mere quibble," I said, plainly unwilling to be detained.

"A great deal may depend upon your attitude to this question," Lamiel went on, with the customary slow deliberation which he seemed capable of applying to profound and trivial utterances alike. "The true answer is that God wills a thing because it is good."

"What follows?"

"This follows. That if God seems to us to command an act, and that act, we are rationally and conscientiously convinced, is not good, then probably we are making a mistake, not about the act, but about the command. God is not, after all, commanding it. Or perhaps it would be better to say—It is not, after all, God who is commanding it."

The Affidavit

> Then, Faustus, stab thy arm courageously,
> And bind thy soul, that at some certain day
> Great Lucifer may claim it as his own.

Marlowe: *Doctor Faustus*

As I left the house, it occurred to me that Lamiel's final comment might be interpreted as referring to my present situation. What was he thinking? And how much did he know? My mind wandered back over his scattered remarks made during the morning, seeking a possible clue to his attitude. But I soon checked myself. I knew enough psychology to realise that moral and theological generalisations could always be given a twist so as to make them especially applicable to one's particular personal situation. How easy it was in church, when the sermon was sound, to imagine that its lesson was specifically directed to oneself, in criticism of one's recent behaviour!

I determined to keep a clear head, and began to fix my attention on the comfortably solid surroundings; the shop windows on my right, and the cars, lorries and buses streaming past me on the left. I gave myself a mental pat on the back for having brought an umbrella, for the scattered clouds of the morning, which had provided pleasing moments of coolness during our sunny walk, had thickened since lunch and now almost covered the sky. Sure enough, as I crossed the railway and started to stride down the High Street, a slight drizzle began to fall. Within ten minutes I had found Coffer standing by the stone steps at the foot of the Honeycross, and looking, I thought, strangely agitated.

"Let us find a quieter place," he said. "We can scarcely hear ourselves speak for the traffic here."

He led me down a side road into the park. Here we sat down on a bench and Coffer began to speak with considerable feeling.

"Events have moved more quickly than I anticipated. I am urgently required back in ...back home above. You must excuse my emotion. You can have little idea of the urgency—the sadness—of the business which calls me away."

The eyes were tragically creased again, and the forehead fell a trifle forward.

"Much is at stake. Many souls are in need. It is a crucial moment in the spiritual career of some well-loved fellow creatures. I must not, cannot delay my departure. Yet neither must I leave my work here unfinished, returning with no clear decision on the case of Lamiel. It is a cruel dilemma. I dare not sacrifice the spiritual needs of others to my natural desire for reaching a decision about Lamiel only after prolonged and careful study."

He raised his hand to his brow and slowly shook his head from side to side, obviously perplexed and unhappy at the calls upon him.

"If I can be of any help..." I began, a little bewildered.

"No," he said. "No. It would not be right to ask you to commit yourself to a duty so painful....And yet," he added reflectively, "perhaps you are even firmer in will and more courageous in resolution than I

think....Have you made any further observations of
Lamiel's behaviour?"

"He appeared a little odd this morning," I said.
"Not his usual direct and cogent self. He said several
things which didn't seem to connect, as though he
were distracted from his actual environment."

"Ah, a lack of grip, a failing of staying-power. It is
as I thought. Yet how I wish it were otherwise. He
cannot be given a recommendation."

"It's too early to say that," I said. "All I mean is that
he seems to have something on his mind, and it makes
him appear distracted and inconsequential."

"That is sufficient. The judgment is an honest,
clear-headed one, arrived at in charity. It is better to
clinch it formally before the mind is clouded by sentiment."

He put his hand into an inside pocket and drew out
an imposing-looking document.

"It is a matter of spiritual life or death that I should
take my leave. Yet I am not permitted to return
empty-handed. It is good to know that duty can and
shall be done, however painful. I see that we have
both made up our minds about Lamiel's capacities.
While respecting his good intentions, we are both
aware that he lacks those qualities which would justify
a recommendation to promotion. All that remains is
that our judgment should be duly and formally regis-
tered on paper. I have here an Affidavit. If you will be
good enough to accompany me to a Commissioner for
Oaths, and append your signature to this document,
the whole case will be closed and you can forget all
about it."

"May I look over it?" I asked.

But Coffer did not hear me. He was looking at his
watch.

"Powers Rejected!" he cried, jumping up. "There is no time to lose. Come along."

Whether he exercised some extraordinary power over me I do not know. But in a few moments I was walking again through the city at his side, his arm locked in mine, and I felt that I was being hustled unwillingly and unpremeditatedly into a course of action which required to be pondered.

"The document—" I began.

"A mere transcript of what we have been thinking and saying: of no special significance in itself, but a necessary formality. It's a mass of legal jargon. Like you, I regret that these formalities are necessary. Like every intelligent man, I despise them even as I make use of them. That is the proper attitude to formalities. We must treat them for what they are—mere operations of machinery, to be set in motion without undue seriousness. The whole procedure is an archaic affectation. The purposive man has something better to think about than the drab conventionalities and inevitable insincerities of legal declarations. We can leave the professional lawyer to treat this stupid jargon with the seriousness proper to a high vocational pursuit. You are absolutely right to shrink from contract with the whole silly and sordid business of sworn affidavits. I admire you for it. The thing is not worth a glance of serious attention. The wise man signs and forgets. I may say that, if I had had my way, this kind of obsolete procedure would have been eliminated from heavenly affairs long ago. But there it is. The mind of officialdom does not easily shake off the fetters of traditional practice, however empty and meaningless that practice may have become. We must humour authority in its little weaknesses."

The stream of his talk flowed over me, and I real-

ised with a jerk that I was neither digesting nor weighing his remarks. A mental fog seemed to cloud my
brain. I felt fuddled, unhappy and, in some way,
trapped. I was being rushed into something from
which I felt an undeniable inner revulsion.

"The text, as I say, is unbelievably silly and unread-
ably verbose. But what it amounts to is just this. You
declare yourself unable to recommend Lamiel for a
post of higher authority. Now this may sound sweeping, but it is perfectly understood above that formal
declarations fail to take into account the subtleties,
qualifications, and hesitancies which naturally mark
all human judgments. All that will be appreciated. It
will not be assumed that you have pondered every pedantic clause of the formal jargon. I can assure you
that the general reaction above will be one of unquali-
fied admiration for your reliability and clear-headed-
ness in reaching a definite decision, and for the selfless
devotion to truth which you have shown, even at the
cost of personal pain."

We stopped at the door of the solicitors, Clapp and
Quintin. I gripped the iron railing by the gate to prevent myself from being hustled inside.

"I must take a glance at the document," I said.

He looked at me with a sudden sadness in his eyes.

"I am reluctant to dwell on the fact that you appear
to distrust me," he said, "for I think of more important
matters—the souls crying out in spiritual distress
which I have been recalled to alleviate. It is their
speedy succour which your wilfulness obstructs."

He looked grave, and I was vastly uncomfortable.
Yet something told me that the headlong rush to an
unconsidered end just had to be halted, whatever the
pleas of urgency. The whole business had earlier

smacked of intrigue, and I felt that its latest developments just had to be thrown into perspective. Against what? A dozen half-formulated ideas tumbled through my head, a jumble of impressions hazily suggestive of a momentous error. On the brink of a formal affirmation, sworn and delivered, I knew that these impressions cried out for cool analysis: Coffer's lack of calmness; Lamiel's imperturbable confidence; the mystery of Coffer's relationship to Julian; Lamiel's strange innuendoes this morning. I gripped the railing more tightly and tried to speak calmly.

"It is stupid perhaps, but I always look over documents before signing them."

With a polite nod of the head Coffer handed me the affidavit. I let go of the railing in taking it, and straight-away he thrust his arm through mine again and hustled me into the solicitors' waiting-room. I unfolded the document, as we stood together just inside the door, and I began to read.

I swear by Almighty God that I ....
of ....
have had the behaviour of the Angel Lamiel under surveillance during his sojourn among men, and that, having due regard to the solemnity of the occasion and to the sacred obligations to speak the truth always in charity, I now declare judgment upon him in these terms:

FIRST: That he is unfit to fulfil the functions of Angelic Guardianship by virtue of the deficiencies named hereafter.

There was no need for me to read further. I knew at once that I could not sign. The words became a blurred mass before my eyes as I strained mentally for the right thing to say.

"It is altogether too formal and definite," I said. And indeed it was. A few hazy criticisms of Lamiel's lack of tact, originality or independence were one thing. An outright formal declaration of his angelic deficiencies was another thing.

"It is a mere record of what you have already agreed to," said Coffer coldly. "Formal declarations inevitably exaggerate. Formality is exaggeration. You have made clear to me what is your view of Lamiel. Where this document goes I go too. It will be interpreted in accordance with my explanations. Have you not found a comparable degree of exaggeration in all the legal documents which you have signed?"

It was true that I had. I nodded and refolded the affidavit, holding it loosely in a fit of hesitation. Coffer quietly took it into his keeping again as I tried to clear my head on the subject. Thus bemused, he took me by the arm again, and soon we were climbing the stairs together to the solicitor's office on the second floor. I had climbed these stairs once or twice before on important occasions in my life. For one thing, Clapp and Quintin had handled the legal side of my house purchase for me. Conscious of a different kind of momentousness in the present situation, I paused thoughtfully outside the office door and gently disengaged my arm from Coffer's.

"I see what you mean," I said. "I expect you're right about Lamiel. And I think you've got hold of my own views properly. But the official quality of this document..."

"A triviality," said Coffer. "You know just how significant a mere document is in your own affairs. Measure thereby what it represents to me who—" and a frightening deliberateness suddenly slowed and quietened his utterance—"who, with a wave of the hand, could whisk you from the earth."

I knew it was true. I hoped it wasn't a threat. But Coffer's calm, piercing eyes seemed to contain the menace of unmeditated possibilities. I shrank from him, and my back pressed uncomfortably against the grill gate of the lift shaft. My voice trembled as I tried to explain myself.

"There is a difference between voicing tentative opinions and committing oneself by oath to formal declarations on paper."

From the deep blackness of Coffer's eyes a penetration seemed to reach out and search my soul. And, for the first time, I became acutely aware of a mysterious unearthly hostility.

"There *is* a difference," he said slowly, his fixed gaze streaming into my cowering eyes. "There is a difference between pondering an act and performing it, between resolution and execution."

And then he added something which set me shuddering with dread.

"Moreover there is an interval between the word of condemnation and the falling of the axe. It is painful; but sometimes it is brief."

As I shuddered back against the door of the lift, a few strands of my hair got caught in the iron network. There was a jab of pain as I shifted my head, and I raised my hand to disentangle the hair. As I did so, Coffer made a sudden lightning movement which flung open the door of the lift, almost knocking me off my feet. As I stumbled, he shoved me into the lift and clanged the door. Before I knew what was happening, the lift was in motion and I was descending alone.

I dropped past the first floor and the ground floor

and waited for the basement. It didn't come. The lift seemed to gather speed in the darkness. Then I suddenly began to wonder whether it was moving at all. How could it be? I shook myself and blinked at the impenetrable blackness. I jumped on the lift floor, trying to judge whether there was solid ground beneath it. Each jump gave me a sickening feeling of inner disintegration in the pit of my stomach. There was certainly no solid ground beneath me. I had the feeling of being suspended in mid-earth; but a strange, low whistle suggested that the lift was moving at a tremendous speed

"There is some devilry in this!" I said aloud.

How right I was.

The Hellish Way of Life

It is not in the sensual animal nature of man's constitution that the origin of evil lies, but in his will to break down the barrier of creaturely relative freedom and substitute for it divine absolute freedom.

EMIL BRUNNER: *The Scandal of Christianity*

When I stepped out of the lift and closed the door behind me, I was astonished to see that my lift shaft terminated alongside several others. At least my first impression was that there were several. My second impression was that there were dozens—perhaps a hundred or more—ranged around the circular walls of a vast dome-shaped building, which was apparently a gigantic underground lift terminus. All around me people were issuing from lift doors. I saw many of them stand for a few moments in bewilderment. Then they began to move in the same direction as the great crowd of their predecessors, converging on a section of the circle around us where the ring of lift doors was broken, and where there was evidently a way out.

The place was unbearably noisy. Quite apart from the buzz of excited talk in the immediate vicinity, I could distinguish the roar of underground trains and the rumble of escalators in the distance. Nearer at hand, ascending lifts set off with a noise like that of an air-raid siren screaming the All-Clear, while descending lifts reversed the music before crashing to a standstill. The clatter of lift gates added another touch of

variety to the din. And above it all a number of con-
cealed loudspeakers relayed an excruciatingly worn
recording of a march, performed by a brass band. It
was some relief, therefore, when this music came to a
sudden stop, and the words of an announcer caused
the crowd to stand still for a few moments and listen.

"This is the Central Lift Terminal. This is the Central Lift Terminal. Welcome to Hell. We offer you a
cordial greeting on your arrival in this, the most misrepresented corner of the universe. Welcome to Hell.
There are no terrors here. Hell is fine. Hell is free. Its
gates are open to all. Proceed down the escalators and
follow the coloured lights."

I am no linguist, but I recognised the repetitions of
this message in French, German, Italian and Spanish
among the sequence of largely incomprehensible announcements that followed. The announcements did
not create any great surprise, to judge from appear-
ances. There was no great fuss. Looking back on those
minutes when I gradually edged myself nearer to the
escalators, I feel it necessary to emphasise what now
seems a remarkable fact. I did not feel very upset or
dismayed at learning that I was in Hell. All that came
later. For the present there was something about the
surroundings which made it impossible to feel worried. It was all so normal and familiar. I do not know
whether this was partly due to the similarity of the
place to the London Underground; but it was certainly in part due to the fact that there was a general
air of efficiency. One sensed that things were well organised and everything under control. One was content to move with the crowd and await what the vast
machine had in store.

Eventually I found myself packed tightly amongst

others on one of the eight parallel escalators, all moving downwards. No one tried to walk down the moving stairs. Everyone was content to be carried. At the
bottom several corridors awaited us, leading out from
a great rectangular hall. An array of illuminated no-
tices made it easy to choose the right one. Indeed it
was only necessary to find a notice in the English language.

> U.S.A. Follow the amber light.
> United Kingdom. Follow the red light.

Now I understood why the lower hall looked like a
section of the Blackpool Illuminations; for there were
lights of every colour, reaching out in lines from the
central notice board. I soon found my corridor; but I
had to halt again. A queue had formed in the entry.
Naturally, I attached myself to the back. It would
have been possible to walk straight past it down the
corridor, but no one was doing so; and I didn't want to
miss anything. I asked the man in front of me what it
was all about, but he had no more idea than I.

"I always join queues," he said. "Habit, I suppose.
They must be giving something out."

And sure enough they were. The queue soon began
to move. And we came in sight of a man in a green
uniform, looking like a bus conductor, who was dis-
tributing little paper booklets.

"No need to ask questions," he was saying as we
came up. "Everything is explained in the book here.
Follow the red light."

"You're busy," said the man in front of me, as he accepted his booklet.

"Always the same at this time," said the official.

"Rush hour this is. And a busy season too. Summer Sessions in full swing up top. They pour 'em down like water in the hot weather. Makes 'em bad-tempered, I suppose."

I took my booklet in my turn and lost no time in examining it. *Beginner's Guide to Hell* it said on the title page. Immediately inside it said—"Keep this book beside you during your first weeks in Hell. It is especially designed to clear up the beginner's difficulties." Words already familiar followed:

"Welcome to Hell, the most misrepresented corner of the universe. Hell is fine. Hell is free. Its gates are open to all. Lay aside your prejudices. BE YOURSELF, and you will soon learn to respect our Hellish Way of Life.

N.B. ON ARRIVAL consult the section headed PRELIMINARIES on page 5."

I turned to page five and read:

PRELIMINARIES.
Follow the red light. Proceed to platform 13. (All red light corridors terminate at platform 13.) Your Reception Centre is the Station Hotel in the city of HAWK, capital of the British Zone. Entrain for HAWK. (All trains from platform 13 go to HAWK.)

This was simple enough, and I was soon seated in a crowded train, rather relieved to be off my feet and able to survey my fellow travellers in comfort. They seemed to be of all ages and of all social classes, and indeed, except that there were no children, what you would call a typical cross-section of the community. No one was in dirty working clothes. All were decently dressed; but it was easy to distinguish the worker in his striped shirt and ill-cut Sunday suit from the man of means and taste who was accustomed to wear good clothes. The women, as is usual in such circumstances, were less easy to classify. The man on my left appeared to be a city gent. At any rate he wore black and a Homburg, and carried a rolled umbrella. He turned to me, looked me up and down, and decided to speak.

"Rather stuffy in here."

"Yes," I said.

"I suppose we ought to expect that." He laughed and then added, "Were they decent to you at the trial?"

"The trial! I haven't had one."

"Really," he said. "You surprise me. I thought everyone had had one. All the people I've spoken to have....I say," he went on after a pause, "you must have had a pretty hectic career, what!"

A slim, white-faced young lady with angular features and predatory eyes, who was strap-hanging immediately in front of us, overheard this and joined in the conversation.

"He probably had nothing of the sort," she said. "No hectic career, I mean. That's what I can't understand. For everyone I have talked to is thoroughly respectable—in the right way. You won't find a criminal among them: that's my impression. Frankly, the whole organisation is topsy-turvy. It's as I expected. They don't *try* to understand you. Can you wonder that they send everybody to the wrong place?"

"But didn't you want to come here?" asked the city gent, in apparent surprise.

"I *didn't*, originally," she said. "But of course I've changed my mind since I've seen how things are. The company is tons better down here." She lowered her voice to a stage whisper. "See the old lady in the bon-

net. That's Mrs. L. J. Hunmanby-Fenwick. She's right
out of the top drawer. And no side at all. Quite charm-
ing. It was the riff-raff who got away with it and went
above. That's why I've changed my mind. I know too
many of them. I wouldn't be seen dead with them."

"Nor will you," said the city gent with a laugh.
"You're quite right, however. As for me, I never
wanted anything but to come here. I told them so at
the trial. And I must say, they respected my convictions, even though they couldn't be expected to sympathise with them. All the same, there was something
very odd about the end of my trial. I'd made it clear
that I preferred Hell to Heaven, and yet they didn't
seem to be able to decide about me. Then a ridiculous
thing happened, which just shows how topsy-turvy
things are. The judge said—'You say you prefer Hell to
Heaven. Suppose you are given, not two, but three
possibilities to choose from. Listen to them and tell me
which you choose. One: to go to Heaven. Two: to go to
Hell. Three: to go to Heaven temporarily, with the op-
tion of moving to Hell if you find it uncongenial.'
Well, I'm an open-minded fellow, and willing to try
anything once, so long as I'm free to reject it. So I
said—'In that case I'll have number three.' And then
the craziest thing happened. The judge said—'That is
final. You go to Hell.' "

The young lady laughed a good deal at this story.
She obviously enjoyed laughing in public, probably
because it gave her the opportunity to set her prominent breasts shaking. A bald-headed man sitting opposite us looked up with an audible grunt. He had
somehow brought his copy of the *Daily Mirror* with
him, and was cool enough to be engaged now in com-
pleting his study of it.

"Unworkable," he said. "The system's unworkable. I always said it was. So I'm not surprised. This division into black and white, I mean. Life just isn't like that. It fails to take into account the subtlety of the human being's inner life. To anyone who has studied these things, the attempt to apply a rigid system of classification to men and women is quite ludicrous. The whole idea was unworkable from the start. I tried to explain this at the trial, but I was crudely shouted down. It's shocking, quite shocking, to see responsibility put into the hands of creatures quite ignorant of psychology."

"There'll be a change," said the young lady. "There'll just have to be. They can't stay forever at this elementary stage."

The bald-headed man nodded dubiously.

"It would take an awful lot of doing to clean things up. You'd have to start right at the beginning, and teach them their A.B.C.'s."

The conversation was broken off, for a moment later the train came to a standstill in a brightly lit station. A loudspeaker blaring out—"This is Hawk. This is Hawk. Alight here for Reception Centre"—caused us all to leave the train and renew our pursuit of red lights. Then, at last, after devious wanderings through white-tiled corridors and two ascents by escalator, we found ourselves out in the street at ground level. Facing us, across the road, stood a huge building which looked like a gigantic Victorian town hall. A long colonnade stretched out to left and to right, and the queue of humans, already forming between two of the massive columns, looked absurdly diminutive by contrast.

Even here, as we queued for admission to the Station Hotel, we could not escape the loudspeakers.

"Welcome to the British Zone. Hell is fine, and the British Zone is finest of all. Welcome to Hawk, the Briton's home from home."

Announcements like this, interspersed between snatches of music, prevented us from thinking and worrying as we moved slowly into the building. Once inside, we came in turn before another man in green uniform at a reception desk. We signed our names in a book and were each given a numbered bedroom key. We were also instructed to gather together in the ball-room next morning for breakfast.

The place turned out to be rather like an enormous commercial hotel. That is to say, it appeared to have all the essential features of a hotel and none of the extras and refinements which give a hotel character. There was too much green paint and linoleum about the place, and there was a tedious economy in the use of space. One didn't come across cosy, odd-shaped lounges in unexpected corners; and they are, after all, one of the things that give hotels individuality and charm. Moreover there was no bar. At least I couldn't find one; and I soon wearied of roaming about the painted corridors in search of something which might serve as a homely focus. I retired to bedroom number 239 on the fourth floor. Sitting down there, away from the noise, I suddenly realised how tired I was. I realised too that, throughout the last few hours, I had been prevented from thinking. The efficient reception machine had seized me and manipulated me, always keeping me just sufficiently occupied to prevent me from taking stock of the situation. The net result was a kind of fog in the mind and a numbed unresponsiveness in the feelings. I got ready for bed, and settled

down between the sheets with the *Beginner's Guide*
for company.

The Hellish Way of Life

BE YOURSELF

This motto sums up the spirit and ethos of Hell, which
have made it what it is today.

More explicitly the principles of Hell have been formu-
lated in the famous SATANIC CHARTER.

This Charter lists the Five Fundamental Rights of Man.
It is the bulwark of Hell's freedom and the inspiration of
Hell's resistance to tyranny and oppression.

I.   The RIGHT of every man to possess his own soul.
II. The RIGHT of every man to develop and express his own
     individuality without inhibition or restraint.
III. The RIGHT of every man to say what he thinks about
     anything at all.
IV. The RIGHT of every man to believe what his own intui-
     tion dictates and to worship accordingly.
V.   The RIGHT of every man to be sole judge of his own
     actions.

These Fundamental RIGHTS confirm the FIVE FREEDOMS OF
MAN to which they correspond:

Freedom of Soul; Freedom of Development; Freedom of
Expression; Freedom of Worship; Freedom of Judgment.

It is not difficult for you, brought up in civilised twentieth-century Britain, to adjust yourself to the philosophy of
Hell. Your education has, in many cases, been based upon
our own Hellish principle of Freedom of Development.
Your cultural and social environment has trained you to
shrink from the spiritual and intellectual tyrannies with
which we are at war. Nevertheless the enemy is not inactive
in the country you have left behind. It is therefore necessary
to pinpoint some of the major dishonesties upon which his
propaganda is based.

You have been taught by the Celestial Propaganda Machine that Hell is the home of evil and misery. There is no

need for us to argue about this fantastic allegation. We can safely allow facts to speak to you for themselves. Hell is a democracy, which stands four-square against the insidious totalitarianism of Heaven. For in Heaven man's basic freedoms are outraged. In the Celestial Kingdom no man is allowed to differ from the established government in opinion, or to oppose it in action. Every inhabitant is required to hand over his own soul to the State authorities for a conditioning process which they have the the hypocrisy to call *Salvation*. Every inhabitant is subjected to powerful psychological intimidation until his will is absolutely adjusted to the dictates of authority. The process of mental softening-up leads to a state of mechanical servility which they call *Regeneration*. Few men have been lucky enough to escape and tell the world what methods are used in these inhuman processes; but there is evidence of persistent questioning by third-degree methods, which weaken the victim's resistance until he yields in a state of hysteria, technically known as *Conversion*. There is also, on celestial admission, frequent use of drugs, known as *Sacraments*. These dispose the mind to acquiescence and subdue the will to unthinking obedience, whilst exciting the victim by hallucinatory illusions.

We do not wish you to believe that your fellow human beings in the Celestial Kingdom are all evil. There is no need for us to imitate the Celestial Hierarchies by indulging in clumsy propaganda, which exaggerates to the point of absurdity, and relies upon the cynical dictum—*The greater the lie, the more credulous the victim*. No, we shall tell the truth, even about our enemies. We can afford to do so. Your fellow human beings in the Celestial Kingdom are the victims of their government, which forcibly moulds them to a pattern, deceiving them with false promises of coming prosperity and bliss. We have nothing against the innocent inhabitants of the Celestial Kingdom. Our hearts go out to them in sympathy. But we are utterly opposed to the régime which deceives and oppresses them. The Cold War is a war of Liberation.

Yet we are accused by the Celestial Hierarchies of nourishing aggressive intentions. With this fantastic theory they predispose our own brothers against us. They dare not let their people know the truth. Look at the facts. They have forbidden their own people to visit Hell. They refuse to allow any but one or two chosen fellow travellers to leave Hell and visit their kingdom. And when they do admit such people, they invariably prevent them from returning home. They veto every attempt to improve mutual relations by interchange of visits. They reject every request for information about citizens of Hell who have managed to obtain Celestial visas in the past, and of whom we have now no trace. Most outrageous of all, they have the inhumanity to allow political differences to destroy the sacred ties of family relationships. Time after time we have pleaded, in the interests of peace and common humanity, that wives in the Celestial Kingdom who are separated from their husbands by the Iron Curtain, should be allowed to rejoin them here in Hell. And what reply do we receive? A mere formal acknowledgement: "Your communication is receiving the consideration it deserves."

We have the moral satisfaction of knowing that, if the Cold War should warm up again into open and bloody hostilities, with disastrous and unthinkable consequences for our own civilisation and theirs, the responsibility for the holocaust will rest squarely upon the shoulders of the ruling clique in the *Sanctum Sanctorum*, who have cynically rejected all our overtures for increased mutual understanding, supporting their foreign policy at home by the flagrant and callous pretence that our intentions are aggressive.

The Cold War is not of our making. We do not believe in the use of intellectual blockades, restrictions upon individual liberty or diplomatic sanctions and reprisals. These are dangerous weapons, apt to get out of control of those who thoughtlessly employ them. Still, less do we believe that actual warfare ever can achieve, or ever has achieved, anything except the impoverishment of those who take up arms on either side. There is no victor in a modern war. We have no right to risk the civilisations so laboriously built up, on their side and on ours, by putting to use the terrible weapons which science has now placed at our disposal. We stand therefore for the policy of improved relations by free and frank negotiations. Around the conference table we can talk as equals. There, if anywhere, lies the hope of an end to the meaningless strife which splits the universe into two great power blocks, forever given over to mutual suspicion and distrust, facing each other from day to day with the menace of war hanging over them.

Your government in Hell stands for peace by negotiation, carried on in an atmosphere of mutual trust and toleration. We have no wish to interfere with the right of the celestial inhabitants to establish and work their own system of government in freedom from external threat or interference. But we demand the same right for ourselves. Democracy is our choice. Totalitarianism is theirs. Yet they too pretend to be democratic, perverting the meaning of a rich and honourable word. They claim that their economic democracy is superior to our liberal and political democracy. But their democracy is nothing more than socialistic materialism. It is true they have achieved an equality of distribution in respect of material things. But of what value is this, when the minds of the people are enslaved by rigid dogma imposed from above, and their lives patterned in a slavish submission of soul and will? It may be that we have here social and material inequalities which they lack above. But this is the price we pay—and gladly pay—for intellectual and moral freedom. Ours is a democracy of the spirit. And we shall never barter our cherished and dearly-bought freedoms of thought, will and soul, for the mess of materialistic pottage which is all that the celestial slave can call his own.

I read; but somehow I didn't take it in very clearly. The whole argument and the phraseology were too like so much that I was accustomed to read without taking it in. I flicked over the rest of the pages and closed the book, determined to sleep. As I did so, my eyes fell upon something on the back page, distinguished from the rest of the contents by being presented inconspicuously in much smaller print.

Notice

It is not to be expected that any man who has gained the privilege of residence in Hell, and who has experienced the broad flexibility of the Hellish Way of Life, will wish to exchange citizenship of Hell for celestial servitude. Nevertheless, in accordance with the terms of the Post-Lapsarian Concordat, we hereby draw the attention of newcomers to the following regulation:

IF ANY MAN, being condemned to Hell, shall soberly and out of his best reason decide that he ought properly to be resident among his brothers above, he shall have the right to apply for a reconsideration of his case by the Angelic Authorities, and if his appeal is approved, a Celestial visa will be forwarded, together with a guarantee of safe conduct to the Celestial Kingdom.

In pursuance of the provisions of the above regulation, the Government of Hell announces that preliminary forms of Application for Transfer may be obtained at your Local Information Bureau. When completed, they should be posted to the Foreign Office for transmission to the Celestial Authorities.

On reflection, this seemed to me to be as hopeful as anything that I had yet come across in Hell. If condemned persons had the right to appeal, surely uncondemned sojourners in Hell had even more right to have their cases properly investigated. I determined to avail myself of this provision at the first opportunity.

Gumption

Reason's lamp (which, like the sun in sky,
Throughout man's little world her beams did spread)
Is now become a Sparkle, which doth lie
Under the ashes, half extinct, and dead.

SIR JOHN DAVIES: *Nosce Teipsum*

When I came downstairs next morning and sought
out the dining room, I was surprised to discover, that
by hellish standards, I could account myself an early
riser. Two or three people were already at breakfast in
the vast canteen, but for the most part the tables were
yet unoccupied. The green varnished walls, the
painted green basket-work chairs and the vulgar glass-
topped tables all combined to give a hygienically uncomfortable appearance. I settled down at a corner
table, took out my *Beginner's Guide*, and awaited
food. Soon a green-uniformed waiter—looking just as
much like a bus conductor as all the other public servants I had encountered—brought me a plate of por-
ridge. He was an old man with lean, pinched features
and a drooping jaw. He was disposed to talk when I
offered an opening.

"I expect you're used to serving raw recruits," I said.

"Been at it a good while, sir," he said. "And not a
bad job by any means. Hours are a bit irregular, but
the pay's reasonable—and there's always a few perks
in a place like this. I've nothing to grumble at. Any
man as is reasonable can find a perch that'll suit 'im

'ere. No need to worry if you're a contented sort.
...But if I were you, I shouldn't take too much notice
of that kind of thing."

He added this last comment in a lower voice, and
pointed to my *Beginner's Guide*, open on the table.

"Oh," I said. "Doesn't it matter, then?"

"Not a scrap. The Powers talk a good deal o' that
stuff. Always on about the Cold War and the fight
against tyranny. Well, it's their job: let them do it. But
most of us just listen and forget. You'll be getting a
good dose of it in the ballroom after breakfast. If you
take my tip, you'll sleep through it. It doesn't mean a
thing."

"The Powers," I said. "That's the devils, I suppose."

"The Angels," he corrected. "They're all right so
long as you keep out of their way. If you *must* get
mixed up with them, don't argue. Just say 'Yes' to everything. You can go away and do what you want then.
It isn't wise to offend them."

"What do they look like?" I asked.

"Tall chaps with white faces and very black eyes.
You can't mistake 'em. They all wear black cloaks
lined with scarlet."

Indeed there was no mistaking them. When we all
gathered in the ballroom a couple of hours later, we
found a small group of these creatures on a platform
at the end of the hall. Three of them made dreary
speeches, telling us how free we were and what a fine
place Hell was.

"Every man," said one, "whatever his talents, has
the opportunity to make his mark here. We encourage
individuality, initiative and enterprise. Every man is
his own leader and his own master. Every man must

find his own inspiration, drive and purpose in himself. That is what Hell means. If you have a taste for servitude, for submission, for external discipline, you'd better apply for a Celestial visa, for you won't be happy here. If you want to be told what you must think, what you must believe and what you must do, then you've come to the wrong place. There is no room here for the narrow man, the small-minded man, the bigot or the intolerant. Hell is for big men with minds unburdened by tradition, with wills unfettered by duties and obligations. Hell is a society of individuals."

There was much more in the same vein, so that it occurred to me to wonder whether perhaps the writers of leading articles on earth were not subject to direct inspiration by the Powers. However, some of them gave us more useful and practical information about how to apply for jobs and seek permanent living quarters. But I was feeling pretty bored when the last speech was announced, to be delivered by a Power named Lather. He had a very big nose and very big ears; and these, in conjunction with the high protruding cheekbones common to all the Powers, made his face look like a collection of bulbous protuberances. Moreover he was the only Power on the platform to be wearing spectacles, and these rested on the various protuberances like a motor-bicycle on a ploughed field.

"It is good of the officiating Powers," he began, "to allow me this opportunity of addressing you and, I may add in anticipation, of using you. I represent the University of Milldyke Junction, an institution, I may say, which guarantees the cultural predominance of the British Zone over every other region of Hell. Our

Research Department is renowned for the scientific thoroughness of its statistical surveys and the comprehensiveness of its analyses of the Public Mind. And it is to assist the Research Department that I invite your cooperation this morning.

"We are at present engaged in a large-scale analysis of the mental capacities of the populace, with a view to discovering the quantitative relationship between Innate Gumption, Functional Initiative and the all-important Disposition towards Social Adjustment. By taking a cross-section of the populace and scientifically measuring their respective degrees of Innate Gumption, Functional Initiative, and Disposition towards Social Adjustment, we hope to be able to throw new light on the problem of Social Misfits, and incidentally to facilitate the rehabilitation of Celestial Dreamers into their actual and factual environment. I may say that Celestial Dreamers, who are overcome by the burden of being responsible for themselves and thus begin to nourish the illusion of Salvationist Utopianism, provide one of our acutest sociological problems. I'm sure you will be happy to assist us in clearing the ground for a new remedial approach to these unfortunate victims of maladjustment.

"After you have settled down, you will be asked to undergo tests in measurement of your Functional Initiative, and later of your Disposition to Social Adjustment. This morning you will oblige us by taking a test designed to measure your Innate Gumption. The less learned among you may be surprised to hear that it is possible to measure so elusive a quality as gumption. And the learned, who have experienced university research on earth, may well be astonished to discover how far we in Hell have left the earth behind in this kind of scientific analysis. Let me assure you that the Measurement of Ability is Hell's own speciality. We are absolutely unrivalled in every field of psychometric theory and practice. We can justly claim the honour of being first in the field in every kind of statistical analysis and quantitative survey. The technique was invented here, and its early and rich exploitation represents our most original contribution to learning and our most far-reaching cultural advance.

"Gumption, I should explain to the uninitiated, is the formative principle of all activity involving the mind. It has been variously defined as *Capacity to use capacity*, *Ability to be able*, and, more wisely I think, as *Potential inability to be mentally inoperative*. There is something to be said for all these definitions of Gumption, though all alike are open to criticism too. I should myself prefer to define Gumption as the *Raw Material of Unrealised Potentiality*, or better still, perhaps, as *Potential Potentiality*. For Gumption is not knowledge, not skill, not talent, not wisdom— though it is the *sina qua non* of all. Nor is it simple potentiality. Rather it is the undefinable prerequisite of potentiality; the thing that makes it possible for possibilities to realise themselves at the mental level; the very spring of that capacity so to energise potential ability that it issues in the direct possibility of that mental change which we so glibly call *thought*."

Two of the Powers on the platform coughed gently. But Lather was now well and truly launched.

"I do not wish you to visualise this elusive raw material of potentiality as possessing a *thinghood* in itself. There is nothing so concrete as a *whatness* about Gumption. To draw an analogy from the mechanical world, let us say that your mind is a car and you are the driver. Gumption is not the engine, not the pistons, not the steering, nor the gears. Nor is it the petrol. It is not even the petrol pump that supplies the fuel. Nor is it the garage mechanic who works the pump, causing the fuel to be poured into your machine. Rather Gumption may be compared to the lady in the cash desk who, by receipting last month's bill, ensures that you shall not be turned away unserved— ensures that the whole machinery of supply shall work efficiently towards the fueling, and ultimately the smooth running, of your car."

"Thank you very much," said one of the Powers, rising quickly to his feet, as Lather paused for a breath.

"One word more," said Lather, forestalling him. "I must explain that every man has a G. Q. or Gumption Quotient. This is the numerical representation of this Gumption Potential and is arrived at by the following formula.

$$G.Q. = \frac{M.A. \times 100}{C.D.}$$

M. A. is the Mark Attained in the test. C. D. is the Chronological Date of your birth. This latter has to be taken into account in order to ensure that the products of more advanced civilisations are not given an unfair advantage in the survey."

"I am sure we are all deeply indebted to Professor Lather for this concise explanation," said the interposing Power, hurriedly leaving no time for more. "You will assemble here for the Gumption Test after a quarter of an hour's break."

To be honest, it was the Gumption Test which fi-

nally decided me how to spend the rest of the morning. When I had finished my paper, I went straight to
the Reception Desk and asked the receptionist the way
to the Local Information Bureau.

"Just round the corner in the square," he said,
pointing out the direction. "And if I were you, I'd
think it over before going there."

"Why?" I asked.

"I've seen your type before. Straight off in search of
a visa without stopping to ask what there is to gain.
Let well alone. You'll only run your neck into trouble.
You won't get out. They very rarely let anyone even
apply. Not that they force you. But they have a way of
arguing."

"One can but try," I said. "There's nothing to lose."

"Isn't there! There's your career here to consider.
And they'll see that it's not very brilliant, if you start
off by trying to get out."

"But surely," I said, "we are free to make our own
careers, applying for what jobs we choose."

"We are and we aren't," he replied. "Nobody ap-
points a man to anything without a discreet word to
the Powers. No compulsory direction, of course, but it
isn't wise to reject their advice." He lowered his voice
and leaned over the desk towards me. "How do you
think they find men to work the mines and handle the
sewage?"

"I didn't think of that."

"It's simple enough. You find yourself turned down
for every job you put in for, till you're on your beam
ends. You'll take anything then."

I left the hotel somewhat shaken in my decision.
Was the risk worth taking? The prospect of an eternity
in the coal mines or the sewage works was dismal in-

deed. Far better, surely, to keep my name free of suspicion and put in for a job at Milldyke Junction University. At least I should there be doing congenial work....Or should I? The frustration of being involved endlessly in meaningless statistical surveys and psychometric research would surely be as unthinkably drab and wearisome as perpetual coal-heaving. Moreover, it would be so much more futile than coal-heaving. There was at least a point and a purpose in mining coal. The work could be rationally justified. It produced coal. While Milldyke Junction University specialised in the Measurement of Ability....I shuddered in recollecting the phrase. I had had enough of measuring ability. It was the very thing that had brought me here. I strode firmly into the Information Bureau and consulted the bus conductor in the Enquiry Office.

"May I have a preliminary form of Application for Transfer?" I said.

"Can't be done." He nodded his head gravely.

"But it says here in the regulation..." I began.

"Oh, yes," he laughed. "They *can* be obtained here, theoretically. We've got some all right. But not for distribution—except on the Boss's orders."

"He's a Power, I suppose?"

"He certainly is."

"Well, may I see him?"

"Phew! You're a stubborn one, you are. Prepared to go to any lengths, are you? All right; but don't say I didn't warn you. Where's your Condemnation Card?"

"My what?"

"The thing they gave you after the trial."

"I haven't got one. Never had a trial."

"Satanic Powers! No trial. A Direct Damnation!

Why, you haven't the chance of a snowball in the fire. D. D.'s are our untouchables so far as the Celestial Authorities are concerned."

This was dismal news indeed, and I was on the point of making a dejected withdrawal, when a bell rang and the official picked up the phone at his elbow. I could hear every word.

"I'm going off for an early lunch if everything is clear. Have you anything for me to deal with?"

"No sir...well, that is, only a very simple matter, I think, sir."

"What is it?"

"A fellow here seeking a transfer form, sir. A D.D., I'm afraid, sir."

Laughter crackled harshly in the receiver and my dejection reached a new depth.

"All right. Send him in."

"Very good, sir."

Jaffer

By these thoughts I was again sunk down and choked;
yet not brought down to that hell of error (where no
man confesseth unto Thee) to think rather that Thou
dost suffer ill, than that man doth it.

ST. AUGUSTINE: *Confessions*

Thus it was that I came to meet Jaffer, whom,
please God, may I never meet again! His low sloping
forehead met the back slope of his bald head at a central egglike apex. The total effect of this odd crown
above the distinct diabolical cheekbones was that of a
disporportionately shallow roof on a bare-walled
house. I say bare-walled, because the eyes resembled a
couple of third-story windows, shadowed absurdly by
the roof. I have seen windows just as black, caught in
the half-light of a slanting sun. Just now they were
grotesquely illumined by an insidious smile.
"You wish to apply for a transfer?"
I nodded.
"Sit down. I must question you."
His eyes looked alternately at me and at the ceiling,
as he spoke in a smooth high-pitched voice.
"Your history we need not enquire into at the moment. In the unlikely event of an application actually
being made, I should of course seek full details about
you from headquarters. Meantime let us concentrate
on your present state of mind."
He smiled, raised his head, lowered his head,

picked up a pencil and twisted it vertically between his thumb and his first finger.

"Give me first just one good reason why you consider yourself misplaced here."

I pondered a second. It was important to make some pretty wholesale and conclusive claim to begin with.

"I am a Christian."

"My dear fellow," he laughed, "of course you are. We are all Christians here. The Zonal authorities have always insisted that the Christian spirit is necessary to support social amelioration and to inspire foreign policy during the Cold War period. I may say that the Christian emphasis upon the dignity of man is the basis of our stand for individual freedom."

I was temporarily nonplussed and, not knowing how to press my claim, I sought further information on this question.

"Have you churches here, then?"

"Oh, no. No churches. Our religion is quite free from the corrupting influence of institutionalism. Ecclesiastical organisations fetter the individual, imposing beliefs externally. True belief springs from sources in a man's own individuality. External bodies, with their traditional dogma and established rites, can but poison and destroy that spontaneous impulse which is the mainspring of genuine religion. Surely you, as an educated Englishman, are fully aware of the insidious and subtle dangers inherent in formal institutional religion? We have sometimes received here clergymen who were anxious to establish official religious bodies in Hell. Whilst sharing our suspicion of dogma and institutionalism, they argued that the social and psychological benefits to be derived from corporate

assemblies would offset the possible dangers of sub-
mitting impressionable creatures to the influence of
suggestive formal acts. But very soon these clergymen
came round to our point of view: they would now be
the first to deprecate any taint of institutionalism, for
the very reason that it cannot exist without doing its
subtle work of practical and dogmatic indoctrina-
tion."

There was a pause, during which the tip of the
swaying pencil was tapped contemplatively against
the thin lips. Then he added,

"Answer one question. Do you wish to be a slave?"

"Certainly not."

"Then I'm afraid you've no case to put forward. An
abject willingness to surrender individual freedom is
the only acceptable condition for entry into the Celestial Kingdom."

I felt there was some twist here. I could see that, in
a sense, his statement was true. But the sense in which
the statement was true, was not the sense in which I
had answered his question with a negative. Yet this
complex reaction defied expression in language.

"I can see," he said, "that I have appealed to your
better nature—to your better judgment. Probably you
now understand things which formerly confused you.
Here in Hell we are friendly to religion—to all reli-
gions. We cherish especially those who have cultivated
that deep sense of inner purity, which is the fine
flower of the religious spirit. We recruit some of our
most useful public figures from religious circles. But
the formal organised body—the Church—no, we
have no use for it."

"It is interesting to hear you say that," I said, a little
surprised at the feeling he displayed. "The contrast

between your attitude to religion in the abstract and your attitude to the concrete ecclesiastical body comes as a surprise."

"My dear fellow, the more human beings think and talk religion, the better, in our eyes—always provided that they don't do anything about it. The cultivation of the religious spirit and of abstract religious interests develops a man's individuality and nourishes his self-reliance; the very qualities we most value down here. But actual membership of a church, with the practices it involves, is disastrous. You see, institutional religion causes people to *do* things. They not only do things: they incur obligations and, in a variety of degrees, cultivate a certain respect and obedience to authority. In other words, the will submits and the individuality is inhibited—disciplined, as they would say above. This is fatal. It plays into the hands of the Celestial Powers and their Satellites."

"I think I begin to understand."

"I should hope you do. It's simple enough. If a man cultivates a vague religious spirit in solitude, well enough. If he talks religion, still that is safe. But if he goes to church, an act of the will is involved. If he joins in public prayer and worship, he associates himself with a body bigger than himself; to that extent he submits his individuality to a corporate activity carried on under authority. Can't you see that all this is simply *obedience*, which saps the independence of the free individuality? Worse still, the churchman probably recites creeds; and however perfunctorily he does it, still there is the act of the will formally committing him. You would be astonished to know what an elementary level of self-committal qualifies a man for the good favour of the Celestial Powers. They have been so unbalanced by our movement and its repercussions, that they seem to set store by nothing except submission.

"Churchmen of one kind win celestial favour because they commit themselves firmly to the authority of an Institution, binding themselves week after week in formal acts and solemn rites. Churchmen of another kind gain celestial favour for a very similar reason, because they commit themselves so firmly to the authority of a Book, binding themselves daily to its injunctions. And the Celestial Powers are incredibly stupid. They seem incapable of stopping to ask themselves—Does this man really *mean* what he's doing? Or does this man really *understand* what he's reading? No, they just clap their hysterical hands and say—There's another will operating in the right direction. There's submission. The rest is easy. The rest we can do."

An idea, previously half understood, dawned upon me with new clarity and force. And I saw the Affidavit for what it was.

"I gather," I said, "that the Celestial Powers are really concerned about formal observances and also about formal declarations."

"Ludicrously so. The formal affirmation of obedience and submission—or, of course, the formal affirmation of spiritual independence and self-reliance—counts far too much in their eyes. The *quality* of the conviction behind it all they neglect. The result is that we get all the really sincere souls down here: all the people who were too honest to commit their minds and wills without the support of their inner feelings.

The people who were humble enough to wait and see, possessing their own souls in patience, tolerantly non-committal about matters of faith and practice—all these the Celestial Powers reject by the dozen. And, of course, this absurd policy must be counted a complete *post facto* justification of our rebellion."

There was no doubt of Jaffer's fervour on this topic. And this fervour was itself instructive. Indeed it explained so much, that I was bewildered at the thought of the many judgments I should have to modify and correct. For one thing, it cast an entirely new light on the nature of Hell's inhabitants. Small wonder they were not recognisable as the world's criminals and down-and-outs. They were simply the people who had never made the first movements of self-committal. Then again, I was astute enough to recognise here a corroboration of much that Lamiel had said, which had seemed at the time too sweeping or too dogmatic. He also had emphasised obedience. Indeed, that was why I was here, learning too late that the issue between Heaven and Hell was at heart summed up in the question of submission.

Now it may appear that I was too easily impressed by Jaffer's argument; but that is not the case. What impressed me was the similarity between his statements and Lamiel's. When two deadly enemies, eternally at war, say the same thing about the very subject of their disagreement, one has the best of reasons for assuming that they are telling the truth. And in this case the truth was not only a revelation—it was a way of escape.

I scrutinised Jaffer's pyramidical head, as he sat there behind his desk, the brow falling forward and the eyes straining up toward the ceiling, as though he wished to explore the merits of the least convenient method of looking upwards. And I began to feel that I had beaten him. I had encouraged his conversation to the point at which he had made it perfectly clear what line I ought to take in applying for a transfer. His eyes fell down upon mine in the silence, and he smiled.

"You have decided to let well alone," he said.

"By no means," I replied. "On the contrary, I have decided to persist with my application."

"Is that so?" he asked, with bland suavity and a touch of feigned curiosity. "I'm sorry. I was too hasty. Have I overlooked some relevant point?"

"You have indeed," I said with rash confidence. "You have overlooked the most important fact of all— the fact that I am seeking proper grounds for a transfer application. Those grounds you have kindly supplied yourself."

"Now, really, have I been so careless as to do that? Dear me." He nodded reflectively and rested his forehead on his hand, as though in meditation.

"I shall apply," I said, "simply on the grounds that I wish to submit to the Celestial Powers. That and nothing more."

Jaffer opened a drawer in his desk, took out a buff form and handed it to me.

"Admirable," he said. "Admirable. You could not have hit upon any formula more calculated to ruin your chances. I shall support you in your application."

The confidence with which he spoke and moved seemed to shake the floor beneath my feet.

"I don't understand..." I stammered.

"My dear fellow, do be logical. You are here because

it is the will of the Celestial Powers that you should be here. If you submit to their will, you stay. The grounds of your application will therefore cancel out the application itself. Your argument will nullify your appeal."

This time I was well and truly beaten. I sat back in my chair and a wave of despair swept over me. I knew there was no possible reply. I stuffed the form into my pocket and held tight my lips in a new intensity of dismay.

"Your case is hopeless," said Jaffer, still smiling, "and now that you have realised it, we can begin to talk. For, believe me, I do not despair of making you a happy and useful citizen of Hell. Once these foolish dreams are finally and utterly laid aside, you will settle down and, judging from the qualities you have already displayed, I should say that you may well rise to a position of eminence amongst us."

I swallowed a lump in my throat, but I could not speak.

"You are a disappointed man. Though you may have already nourished hard thoughts against us Powers, I am prepared to be conciliatory, even indulgent. I want you to find your proper place among us. I shall therefore make arrangements by telephone for you to see something of the University at Milldyke Junction this afternoon. I have no doubt that a visit will whet your appetite for exercising your talents in the academic world. Moreover, as a special indulgence, you shall have the rare opportunity of listening tomorrow morning to a Government debate in which matters of high policy will come under review. This, I am confident, will finally dispose of the stupid illusion which brought you here this morning. Take this ticket, and be at the Government Buildings by ten o'clock."

He handed me a card, on which I read:

Satanic Powers Federal Government
British Zone
Admit one person to Visitors' Gallery
Government House.

I rose from my seat and mumbled a thank-you.

"It has been a pleasure," he said. "Don't forget to look in at Milldyke Junction this afternoon. It's only a bus ride away. You'll feel at home there, I'm sure. Good morning."

Milldyke Junction

If in these feeble beginnings, O Lord, our hearts are
not entirely Thine, let them at least feel that they ought
to be so.

ABELARD: Letter to Heloise

The university reminded me of the hotel, but I find
it difficult to convey exactly what the similarity was.
Let me put it this way. The hotel contained all those
attributes which factually constitute an hotel, but
none of these qualities which provide the "feel" of an
hotel. It was the same with the university. For instance, I was first led by a porter (another bus conductor) across a great quadrangle. That it deserved to be
called a quadrangle the shape and the structure of the
surrounding buildings verified. But it had none of
those qualities which justify the existence of the quadrangle, and therefore the architect might just as well
have left it out. I mean, if four drab factory-like walls
around a bare stone-flagged rectangle constitute a
quadrangle, then this was one. But there was no
charm, no grass, no architectural beauty, no sense of
repose—worst of all, no secure sense of being en-
closed. The very solidity of the walls and the absence
of any shelter round the sides merely emphasised the
fact that one was outside, exposed to the elements. It
was space to be traversed, not ground to be lingered
on.

And when I got inside, the standard green paint, already encountered in the hotel and the Information Bureau, reinforced this impression of characterlessness. The corridor floors were of concrete and the stairways were flanked with iron banisters. If this is a place to study in, I thought, well and good; but it might just as well be a place to make electric bulbs in, to store groceries in, or to die in.

The porter knocked at a green door, indistinguishable from a hundred others except by a number, and then left me to respond to the "Come in" alone. Professor Lather turned at his desk, without rising, and bade me be seated.

"I was expecting you," he said, and then went on writing.

The bulbous face, rather comical at a distance, was thoroughly unpleasant in closer proximity. The nose was badly pock-marked and the ear lobes positively swollen. If only he'd change his steel spectacles for thick-rimmed ones, I thought, he'd make a more presentable job of what is, one must admit, most unpromising material. My eyes wandered to a wooden shield on the wall, bearing a crest in green and gold. The design showed a typewriter surmounted by a megaphone, these articles being encircled by a string of percentage symbols. Underneath ran the motto *In numero vis.*

Lather put down his pen and swung round to face me on his revolving stool.

"In what direction do your academic interests lie?"

"I'm a student of literature," I said.

He shook his head.

"No use here, I'm afraid. We have no faculty of literature—nor of language, for that matter."

"How can you justify their neglect?" I asked.

"Useless and unprofitable studies are not allowed here. The idea of working at a subject without due regard for the practical benefits to be obtained from it—this idea we consider absurd, even criminal. No man has the right to prosecute studies which will not bring material and social benefits to the society he resides in. Every scrap of work done in this institution serves a clear utilitarian purpose. We exclude utterly the study of philosophy, history, language and literature. Literature is especially dangerous—imaginative literature, that is. I say especially dangerous because it exercises a subtler and less open influence upon the mind. In a word, it indoctrinates. Your novels, plays and poems may appear, at first sight, to be mere material for entertainment. But in fact, anyone who regards them thus, seriously underestimates them. In reading them, a man's individuality may succumb to poisonous inhibitions which fetter his growth. He thinks he is just enjoying a tale, when in fact he is unconsciously learning to commit himself in submission to certain codes of thought and behaviour which are encouraged by the Celestials. Imaginative literature insidiously presents a man with values—unreal things outside himself, which he furtively learns to serve, as though they were something greater than he. This is bad. I must not put it too strongly, and I should not like to shock you; but frankly—if you will excuse the word—this is the road to Heaven."

I was about to speak, but he waved his hand in deprecation of any interruption.

"Oh, I know, I know. It is but a step on the road; and many a man has been rescued who has trod far in that direction. Nevertheless, imaginative literature, on the whole, exercises this regrettable influence, all the more regrettable for the fact that it operates at the subconscious level."

"Not all our imaginative writers are your enemies," I said.

"By no means. You have produced recently a pretty good crop of writers who can be exonerated from the charge of insinuating respect for any values at all. Still, you must remember the great mass of literature surviving from earlier, less-enlightened ages, which subtly corrupts the individuality by subduing it. And, in any case, even healthy imaginative literature must be excluded from our courses on the prior grounds of utility."

"What, then, are your main studies here?"

"We have faculties of Sociology, Economics, Psychology, Education, Statistics and Technology."

"No natural science?" I asked, in some surprise.

"Scientific studies are kept in a strictly subordinate place in the faculty of Technology. In the same way, mathematical studies are pursued only within the faculty of Statistics. Both science and mathematics can be dangerous if they are pursued independently, for their own sake. Geared to statistical and technological research, they can be kept under strict control."

"What about Law?"

"No need for it. That kind of thing is in the hands of the Powers."

"I cannot see a place for myself," I said, "in the university as you describe it."

And indeed it sounded more like a technical college than a university.

"Well, you shall take a look at the place, nevertheless," said Lather, rising from his stool.

And he lead me from one lecture room to another,

all, so far as I could see, identical with one another, except for slight variations in equipment. After seeing a dozen or more of these green-walled rooms, I was relieved when he suggested a visit to the library.

"I have shown you what there is to see. In the library perhaps you can browse away an hour or so, and form an impression of the range of our studies."

"You obtain books from the earth?" I asked, as we climbed one more concrete staircase and turned into yet one more bare corridor.

"We do. Our own publications, though qualitatively unrivalled, tend to be specialised, and more elementary books are needed too. We select very carefully from earthly publications. That goes without saying."

We went through a doorway into a smallish room equipped with steel chairs and tables, and littered with scattered newspapers.

"This is our periodicals room—a kind of anteroom to the library proper. You will find one or two familiar journals here," he said, flicking over a pile of papers. "We encourage all students to read the *New Statesman,* for instance. And of course we take *The Times Educational Supplement*: it is so very good when it touches upon religious topics."

He led me through another door into the library itself, and then prepared to take his leave.

"You may browse at will and go when you wish. Psychology and Education are down this side; Sociology and Statistics down the other. For Technology and Economics you must climb the spiral staircase on to the gallery.

"You will find many familiar writers on the psychology shelves: indeed your twentieth-century psychologists deserve to be complimented for their work, which is deeply appreciated down here. There are exceptions, of course, but on the whole we are proud of them. They have done so much to re-establish the autonomy of the individual and to weaken submission to so-called 'objective' values. Then again, they have helped immeasurably in the great work of discrediting the old authoritarian calls to self-transcendence in religious worship and obedience. We are indeed happy to count your psychologists among our most useful allies. Not that your sociologists and economists lag far behind. They deserve their word of praise too. They are so good at shutting off the whole Celestial Order from man's thoughts and calculations; so effective in making him feel the completeness and comprehensiveness of his own show on earth. This is a great thing to have achieved. It destroys that miserable sense of dependence which sets men seeking celestial guidance. Indeed it is difficult to know which body best deserves our thanks—your psychologists, your sociologists or your economists. They have all so admirably contributed to establishing man in self-reliance: they have killed that human illusion of a Divine Purpose seeking to involve man, and a Divine Will yearning for man's submission. However, you can see for yourself what earth's contribution is." He waved his hand in the direction of the shelved walls. "May I say, in parting, that I hope very much to see you permanently established here?"

I thanked him, and he left me. Glancing over the psychology shelves, I saw how right he was. Familiar books and familiar names seemed to stand out among the mass of unfamiliar ones. Not all the books deserved to be called learned. In fact some were distinctly popular. For instance, I picked out a new American volume called *Modern Guide to Modern Parenthood*, by Shoesmith and Symes. It contained the usual chapter headings—"The Ante-Natal Stage," "The Infant's Environment," "The Child in the Family," "The Child becomes a Person," "The Sex Factor," and so on. The thing seemed to be written in a chatty, one might say patronising style, with occasional bursts of technical jargon which stood out incongruously. Apparently the writers wished to assume the role of the family doctor, giving intimate advice. I should have returned the book to the shelves, as typical of a thousand others, were it not that the title of an early chapter promised something novel, and curiosity prompted me to sample it.

THE ANTE-GESTATION STAGE

The *ante-gestation stage* is a phrase now universally used to describe the period in a future mother's life which precedes the actual conception of the child. It has too long been the custom of psychologists and doctors to neglect this important stage, which can have a significant formative influence upon the future citizen. It is no exaggeration to say that the proper care of the mother during the ante-gestation stage is of cardinal importance to the future child. Indeed, if the mother is not properly treated at this stage, one can go so far as to say that there may be no future child at all. Psychological factors are all-important. Plenty of new hats, plenty of evenings out and plenty of good company; these little attentions will help to keep the healthy-minded woman happy during the critical ante-gestation stage. Nor must we forget the father, who at this time needs to be fortified against the future by plenty of good food, tobacco and sleep. Domestic harmony during the ante-gestation stage will make a great deal of difference to your future child: for instance, it will make him a good deal older than he might otherwise have been.

Some wives have asked us—Ought I to take special precautions during the ante-gestation stage? We always advise the contrary. Special precautions are apt to exercise a subjective influence, creating an unnecessary and premature sense of urgency. Continue with your normal life. Just be yourself, as though nothing untoward were in the air.

And now about the future baby. Think of him, at this time, always calmly and without nervous excitement or elation. Be natural about him: do not *fuss* over him. After all, there is really nothing to fuss over just yet, is there? You must prefigure him (or her) in tranquillity and contentment. To do otherwise is to heap up possible trouble for yourself. Psychologists have often traced back the causes of infant bedwetting to the impatience and fretfulness of a neurotic mother during the ante-gestation stage.

Of course, calmness is not the same thing as irresponsibility. No sight is sadder than that of the mother-to-be who is careless and unstable during the ante-gestation phase. At this stage the happy woman should continually call to mind that she no longer exists for herself alone; for another life is one day going to depend upon her own. Another little being is going to share her food, her work, her rest. It is only fair to say that there is controversy in the medical world over the question whether the future mother should eat enough for two during the ante-gestation stage. Food for two, says one eminent authority, is a biological necessity for every married woman. But other experts regard this as an exaggeration. A fairly safe piece of advice is that you should eat enough to satisfy yourself without making yourself sick.

Although the ante-gestation stage has its difficulties for many women, it can be a most satisfying phase—a period of great happiness and quiet fulfilment. Indeed, some wives find the stage so agreeable that they endeavour to remain at it indefinitely. There is a little difficulty here—a verbal difficulty. For if the ante-gestation stage is indefinitely prolonged, so that it never passes over into the ante-natal stage (see Chapter IV *passim*), have we the right to call it the ante-gestation stage at all? In order to differentiate the true ante-gestation stage from the prolonged experience of non-gestation, we shall call the latter the *non-gestation* stage. Now, although the ante-gestation stage is of first importance to us here, the non-gestation stage is a matter of great interest and deserves something more than a passing mention. Non-gestation is by no means uncommon among women; and among men it is the prevailing condition. This is what gives the non-gestation stage its peculiar interest: it provides a link between men and women. Perhaps women in the non-gestation stage are best equipped to deal with masculine foibles and instabilities in a spirit of true sympathy and understanding.

To return, however, to the ante-gestation stage. At this time husbands should treat their wives with especial tenderness and consideration. We shall speak quite plainly to the menfolk on this point. Remember that your wives are going through a most trying phase. Gone are the carefree days of non-gestation, but the days of ante-natal hope, promise and cheap milk are still in the future. In short, this is a stage of transition....

I replaced the book on the shelves, and moved on to the section labelled "The Measurement of Mind." A large volume, issued by a London publisher, and written by a well-known English educationalist, attracted my attention because, though I had seen it universally acclaimed in reviews, I had not yet handled a copy. It was called *Principia Psychometrica*, and had been hailed as the most thorough and comprehensive treatment of psychometric techniques to date. I took it down and read the short Preface.

This book is the product of a lifetime's experience and research. The energy devoted to it will not have been wasted, if the book fulfils the author's purpose of disposing forever of the notion that the mind is anything other than a natural product of the evolutionary process, subject to the same techniques of scientific analysis and experiment that have been so successfully applied to other natural phenomena.

In reaching the end of my labours, I am conscious of debts to many able scholars who have done pioneering work in this subject, and to many teachers who helped me in my early days. In particular I should like to express my gratitude to Professor Lather. I have long lost touch with him. I am not even sure that he still lives. But it was the inspiration and guidance of his teaching, some thirty years ago, which first set me to work in the researches which have now produced their fruits. If this book should come to his notice, I hope he will accept a belated acknowledgment of the power and effectiveness of his teaching. I shall never forget those quiet winter evenings when Professor Lather so generously (and—I may add—so mysteriously) entered our student discussion, to charm our young intellects with the force of his reasoning. If we are now able to study the human mind rationally and scientifically with eyes unfogged by ancient superstition, it is in no small measure due to his teaching. If he has now passed from us, I can but bear testimony that the domination of English education by psychometric studies and practices is his especial and enduring monument.

The book was in two parts. Part I was theoretical, treating of the growth, development, and scientific basis of mental testing. Part II was more practical, giving examples of tests suitable for various ages in measurement of various faculties. On glancing through the contents, I spotted only one remarkable novelty, and that was the serious treatment of mental testing at the infant stage. To this I turned.

Testing the Intelligence of Infants during their first two years

Every parent wants to know as soon as possible what his child's future will be: then he can ensure that the child's future actually *is* that, and not something else. It is not difficult to measure the Intelligence of a child of one or two years. His vocabulary may be limited; but this is really an advantage, for, in testing the Intelligence of older children, differences of verbal equipment are a hindrance. You think you are getting at the child's intelligence (I.Q.) when in fact you are really measuring his Verbal Ability (V.A.). This mistake cannot so easily be made with young children (Y.C.), whose Verbal Ability (V.A.) is usually undeveloped (U.D.). We must remember that Intelligence (I.Q.) is not ability in any given direction (G.D.) but just potential capacity (P.C.) for being able to do things in no direction at all. Of course, we want to know a child's special gifts (S.G.) as well as his general intelligence (G.I.) in order to encourage him to choose the right career (R.C.) with the least possible chance of error (C. of E.). The following two tables will enable you to discover, first, the Y.C.'s G.I. (or I.Q.) simply as P.C. in isolation from the V.A. (U.D.) or S.G. in any G.D.: second, the Y.C.'s S.G. in any G.D. which will largely determine the R.C. and evade the C. of E.

Finally, by putting together the I.Q., obtained from the first table, and the S.G., obtained by means of the second table, you will arrive at your child's T.A.T. (Talent and Ability Total) which determines his all-round H.P. (Human Potential).

I put down the book disconsolately and walked out of the library, more than ever convinced that I did not want to work in the university. I was overcome with mental nausea, and the bilious green paint sickened my eyes and my heart. Possessed suddenly with a shrinking unwillingness to see Lather again, even accidentally, I actually ran down the steps and along the corridor to the main door. And I didn't stop running until I had crossed the flagged quadrangle and reached the dirty, slum-ridden street in which the university buildings were situated. I turned right, up the hill, and watched a succession of horse-drawn brewer's drays, laden with empty barrels, sliding clumsily over the damp glistening cobble-stones towards the brewery just below the university. The road was damp, not with rain, but with mist; a late August mist which seemed to promise an early collapse of summer into autumn.

Did Jaffer seriously expect me to be seduced by the attractions of Milldyke Junction, or was he fully aware of my state of mind and anxious to probe my misery to its depths? Something in the fellow's calmness and something about his bland smile had told me that he intended me the maximum injury. But even the Devil can speak true; and what he had said about my applying for a transfer seemed irrefutable. Without questioning the Divine Omnipotence, I could not deny that I was here in Hell by the will of Celestial Authority. Submission to this will was the only way of salvation: and to submit was to stay.

Yet a sudden gleam of hope presented itself. I recalled the last words Lamiel had spoken to me, before I set out on my ill-considered journey. If God seems to command an act, and that act, we are rationally and conscientiously convinced, is not good; then we are probably making a mistake, not about the act, but about the command. God is not, after all, commanding it. Could this mean that I was not here by Divine Command?...No, the argument fell to pieces, and the new hope was dissolved. Lamiel had been talking about choosing between future courses of action. My dilemma was a present fact. One might dispute whether some future possibility would be in keeping with the Divine Will: but here was a quite different problem; not the problem of a future possibility, but the problem of a present fact. I was already in Hell. I was not a man seeking to discover the Divine Will.

The Divine Will had already manifested itself.

It was meaningless to argue from the fact that my presence in Hell was, in my eyes, a bad thing. It was also a bad thing in God's eyes. So was everyone else's presence in Hell. So was the existence of Hell. You couldn't argue from this that everybody ought to be immediately transported to Heaven. For one thing, people I had met here generally didn't want to go to Heaven. They couldn't be forced from Hell. But I did want to leave. Didn't that make a difference? How could it, when my wanting was a refusal to submit, and submission alone qualified for Heaven?

I got myself into a thorough and miserable mental tangle. But at least I decided again that I would, after all, fill up the transfer form—even if I omitted to fill in the section requiring "Reasons." Yes, that was a good idea. I could put "As God wills" or something to the same effect. That might do the trick.

A moment later I was laughing bitterly for my stupidity and self-centredness. What was the use of putting "As God wills" when it was not a true profession of submission, but a mere device, a trick exploited in the single hope of getting what I myself desired? The very fact that I sent in the form would indicate that my own will to escape was the determining factor, and everything else mere corroborative and subordinate material—deceptive material too.

I was trapped, and the hateful smile of Jaffer somehow presented itself as the symbol of my despair. I determined to think about something else, bought an evening newspaper, and joined the queue for my bus back to Hawk. But, ironically enough, the first thing I read, when I opened my paper on top of the bus, forced my mind back to the tortuous channels from which it was trying to escape.

TWO DIPLOMATS DISAPPEAR
ARE THEY BEHIND THE IRON CURTAIN?

By Our Special Correspondent

It was officially confirmed today that two highly placed
Civil Servants (names withheld for security reasons) have
disappeared. No secret is made of the fact that the two men
were engaged in top-priority secret work at the Foreign Office. It is now widely assumed that they have been lured
away by celestial agents. This probability has produced a
crisis atmosphere in government circles. Well-informed observers admit that there are good grounds for doubting the
loyalty of the missing men. In response to discreet inquiries,
several people have come forward to testify that the diplomats had, on several occasions, made remarks in grave criticism of the government's foreign policy, which it was their
duty to carry out loyally. The crisis is likely to raise again
the whole question of the credentials and reliability of high
officials in the Civil Service. The present widespread belief
that the two diplomats have for long been known to their
acquaintances as fellow travellers, suggests that the Secret
Service is deplorably inefficient.

This discreditable episode will but increase the demand
for more thorough screening of individuals entrusted with
top-level diplomatic work. A government spokesman, questioned this morning, said: "There is no cause for disquiet.
The case in question is an exceptional one. We are satisifed
that our present screening arrangements are in general adequate. We are, however, instituting a full inquiry into the
history of the missing diplomats, and in the event of any serious neglect of duty coming to light, we shall take prompt
and decisive measures."

Asked whether this meant that there was to be no immediate tightening-up of screening methods, he said: "The situation is always fluid. Our security measures are under
constant review." When pressed with further questions
about the possibility of celestial spies having blackmailed
the diplomats, he said: "We are always working under the
difficulty of lacking exact information about the secret intentions of the Celestial Powers. It is certainly within the

range of possibility that the two diplomats have been secretly conveyed above. We shall institute full inquiries through the usual channels. But the government wishes to make it clear that there can be no satisfactory end to these periodical crises, and no easing of international tension, until the Celestial Government abandons its present policy of intimidation and espionage, and allows its representatives to meet ours for a full and frank exchange of views."

I found myself regretting that I had not the qualifications to justify me in applying for a job at the Foreign Office. What hope had I of meeting a celestial spy who might endeavour to blackmail me? I was miserably shut off from any such hope. Looking out of the window, I saw the crowds thickening rapidly on the pavements, as the factories and offices closed for the day. Here and there, as we rushed through the busy streets, I spotted a break in the streams of heads and shoulders thronging the pavements below me. And I noted that usually the erect figure and scarlet-lined cloak of a Power moved between human masses at that point. Men shrank from these Powers. I wondered how many of Hell's human residents would read of the fate of the diplomats with an envious eye.

Membership of the Body

The state of divine union consists in the total transfor-
mation of the will into the will of God, in such a way
that every movement of the will shall be always the
movement of the will of God only.

ST. JOHN OF THE CROSS: *Ascent of Mount Carmel*

I had just sat down to supper in the hotel dining
room, when I was joined by the city gent who had
spoken to me in the train the day before.

"How are you feeling?" he asked.

"Hellish," I said. "Which is presumably what one
should expect."

"I'm sorry to hear that. The place is right enough.
You must adjust yourself and not fret. Hell is what you
make of it, they tell me: and, as for me, I'm going to
make it worthwhile."

He stroked his greying moustache with his left hand
and his thick greying hair with his right hand. Then,
as if anxious not to omit anything, gave a gently decisive flick to each of his greying eyebrows.

"I think I shall take a job in the Civil Service," he
said. "I've made one or two very useful contacts today,
thanks to a few old friends. I was well in with a ring of
really good types in the City, you know—the top-
notch inner circle—and I've got into touch with two
or three of the old-stagers today. They've got their
hands on some good things here too. I might have
known it. It certainly pays to keep in with fellows."

121

"From the City to the Civil Service," I said. "That sounds an unpromising progress."

He laughed.

"It does. You're right there. But here things are not the same as above. You've just got to be in with the government if you're going to get anywhere at all down here. The place is riddled with government controls. A successful business career is out of the question, unless you've got a government job to back it up. Everything centres on government loans and contracts. A Civil Service job will be a necessary second string: the main aim is to get somewhere in the old line. I fancy a bit of trade in Real Estate to begin with. That's always a good stand-by for accumulating a spot of capital. People must have houses, you know. There's definitely a seller's market here—and will be, by all accounts. Immigration is on the up-grade, if that's the right word."

"You haven't any useful friends at the Foreign Office, have you?" I asked. "Because I fancy a job there myself, after reading tonight's paper."

"Oh, the missing diplomats. That's a very funny case, very funny indeed. I was talking to a fellow in the Intelligence about it this afternoon; and he gave me the low-down. Really, there are some pretty shocking things going on above, you know."

He nodded his head gravely and sprinkled salt upon the steak and kidney pie now deposited before us by a bus conductor.

"Much of the evidence is circumstantial," he went on, "but very conclusive nevertheless. And the picture they're building up of political life above is not a pretty one."

"Worse than here?"

"My dear fellow, you don't know you're dead. Up there you're in for systematic torture unless you knuckle under to the last detail from the start. The slightest resistance, and they get to work on you. Weeks of solitary confinement first, to soften you up. Then the questioning starts. No physical torture— nothing so honest as that—but a process of refined psychological intimidation. It's a kind of worrying process. They batter and bludgeon you with incessant questions till you're driven into a perverse kind of self-analysis, when you'll say absolutely anything about yourself. They extract confessions and retractions and self-condemnations. Any sign of resistance, and back you go to solitary confinement to think over your miserable lot. Then, after a time, they start on you again. And they won't leave you alone until they've torn every shred of self-reliance out of you. Everybody succumbs in the end, they say. It's quite impossible for human nature to hold out. The propaganda machinery is so powerful, and the psychological torture is so persistent, that human beings just can't stand up to it. They become grovelling, snivelling creatures, able to talk of nothing but their own miserable weakness and sinfulness. They get to the stage of meeting every request and every suggestion with a plea of utter and contemptible unworthiness to exist. Then the Powers are satisfied. They take their victims and give them proper jobs and publicly announce that So-and-So and Such-and-Such have renounced themselves in absolute submission to the State—only they daren't say 'State': they call it 'the Divine Will.' Let us rejoice, they say, that Tom, Dick, and Harry have succumbed at last, and can in the future wear the badge of full Party-members."

"Do they really say 'Party-members'?" I asked, not a little suspicious of the phrase.

"Something like that. 'Members of the Body,' I believe, is the actual phrase. But it means the same thing. It's a closed circle under totalitarian domination from the *Sanctum Sanctorum*. And you can't get in except by this appalling destruction of your individuality."

"The members choose to submit," I said.

"It's a mockery of free choice. Everything is chosen for you. You've no real freedom, except the freedom to resist; and that they beat out of you. It's a terrible affront to the dignity of man."

"What we really ought to know," I said, "is whether the members are truly happy in the end."

"I daresay they are, in a terribly perverted kind of way. But you can buy happiness at too high a price."

"I wonder if you can," I said sadly.

"No doubt of it. You talk to someone who really knows what goes on up there. For I haven't said half that could be said. There are darker things yet: horrible superstitious rites that make you shudder to think of."

"For instance?" I pressed.

"Well, for instance, they gather periodically for a terrible ceremony associated with the barbarous old myth of the Dying God. It is said that they actually devour the flesh of the slain Victim."

"I can't help thinking," I said, "that we could judge more justly of all these things if someone from their side were to come here and explain."

"They jolly well see to it that nobody gets back here to tell the tale. That's the cunning of it."

He handed his empty plate to the bus conductor,

and received a dish of pink blancmange in its place.

"It all makes one jolly glad to be here. My only re-gret is that I've reason to believe my brother isn't here, and I wanted to see him again. We built up the busi-ness at home together."

"Died young?" I asked.

"Killed in the war," he said. "And the bitter thing was that he needn't have been. Got safely through till nearly the end, and then was fool enough to go and drag a wounded fellow from in front of a machine-gun. Just thoughtless stupidity, I suppose. I expect they got him up top for that."

"Yes," I said. "Perhaps so."

"Well, no good being miserable about it," he added, sucking the last vestiges of pink from his spoon. "We can't all be lucky."

"Maybe your brother now thinks he's the lucky one," I suggested.

"Maybe. I know they're very keen on that kind of thing up there—chucking yourself away, I mean. From what I hear, they don't much mind how you do it, so long as it's sufficiently undignified for their per-verted taste. Of course, there's some excuse for a chap who chucks himself away in the heat of battle, when there isn't time to think things out properly. But to do it in cold blood! To have a perfectly healthy man crawling about and snivelling that he's a worm. Really it makes you sick."

We sipped our coffee and my mind took up its fa-miliar burden, in the familiar way which was now an ever-present torment. That is to say, phrases ran through my head which might suitably be put on the transfer application in order to create the right effect. "I want to chuck myself away because I'm fed up with myself." "I want to be happy at any price, even at the cost of total self-abnegation." "I want to forsake all self-reliance." But it was all to no purpose. I knew, as I framed the phrases, that they would not do. They were just not true. They were so many calculated devices for getting out of Hell and into Heaven. They were thought-out mechanisms for serving my own will. They wouldn't take in a psychologist, let alone a Celestial Power.

"Don't brood," said my companion, shaking me out of my obsession. "Come along with me for an hour in the ballroom. There's a floor-show on tonight."

My first impulse was to decline the invitation. But on second thoughts, I accepted. For what was the point of returning to my bedroom to gloat in solitude over my own miserable dilemma? Better the distraction of a floor-show in Hell, however unattractive that might sound to the regenerate.

Lowbrow and Highbrow

The lure and slavery of aestheticism always indicate the
weakening and even the destruction of the value of per-
sonality, and the turning of one side of man into the
whole. Man makes himself a slave of his partial states,
of the emotional charms which take possession of him.

BERDYAEV: *Slavery and Freedom*

We lit our cigarettes and strolled into the ballroom.
Nor were we too soon, for the seats were almost all occupied, and we counted ourselves lucky to find two
vacant adjacent ones near the back of the hall. Next to
me, on my right, was a fat heavy-faced man, smoking
a cigar and dressed in a loud-striped suit. He wore a
vulgar scarlet tie and smelt of hair oil. I decided that
he must have been a bookie. He was less quick in coming to a decision about me: I felt him eyeing me up
and down for some moments before he spoke.

"A newcomer?"

"Yes," I said. "Aren't we all?"

"You are." He gave a smug grunt of satisfaction.
"But I'm not. Just dropped in for the evening. I happen to live nearby, and I have some good friends here.
They let me know when there's anything worth seeing."

"So it's to be a good show?"

"Should be tip-top. They've got some first-rate
names on the bill."

The lights dimmed and a spot directed our attention to a dress-suited gentleman who was apparently
the compère.

"Ladies and gentlemen, for our first number I have great pleasure in presenting that inimitable cabaret artiste, the incomparable Miranda Max."

The bookie nudged me and became confidential.

"You'll like Miranda. She's the goods. All wrapped up in cellophane."

He laughed immoderately at his own joke, which was explained immediately by Miranda's appearance. For she was dressed in a cunningly contrived costume which, in design, was exaggeratedly Victorian: but it was fashioned of utterly transparent nylon. Since she wore nothing underneath, the total effect was a grotesque combination of nudity and Victorian respectability.

Miranda sang to piano accompaniment. As she did so, she sailed up the gangway between the audience, offering the maximum opportunities for appreciation of her charms. The song itself was not notable—and I doubt whether people took the trouble to note it, being preoccupied with other matters: but the husky voice proclaimed its message in slow long-drawn-out phrases as Miranda sailed among us, swaying her hips, and not only her hips.

> You can see through my little excuses
> To delay you, when we part;
> You can see through my girlish ruses
> But you can't see through my heart.

> You can see through my little caresses
> And the sobs, when the tears start;
> You can see through my evening dresses
> But you can't see through my heart.

After this languid performance, Miranda was

treated to enthusiastic applause and, in response, she added a short piece by way of encore. Although melodically it was in a somewhat less melancholy vein, Miranda gave it the same husky long-drawn-out treatment as before. This style was clearly what made her inimitable and incomparable.

> Why does the pussy-cat keep on purring
> When she's finished her milk
> and there's nothing occurring?
> It don't make sense like most things do;
> And it don't make sense that I keep on loving you.

This trifle accomplished, Miranda swayed off stage to the sounds of hearty clapping, her buttocks glancing from side to side, as from behind a waterfall, in a last dispensation of liberal bounty.

A vastly livelier number followed. A chorus of scantily-dressed female tap-dancers kicked themselves into view and sang a song which smacked rather of the pantomime than of the cabaret. The banal verses were interspersed with bouts of noisy rhythmic clattering.

> They sang us hymns of a place above
> Where there's endless bliss and lots of love;
> But here we are, and it's just as well,
> For there ain't no cares in Hell.

> They told us such beeeautiful things
> Of blessed angels with golden wings;
> But here we are, and life is swell,
> For there ain't no cares in Hell.

> SOLO: The parson pulled a solemn face
> And warned me off this wicked place;
> But here I am—and he's here as well,
> CHORUS: And there ain't no cares in Hell.

SOLO: "Now don't be such a saucy miss!
            You mustn't cuddle and you mustn't kiss!"
            But I cuddled and I kissed and down I fell,
CHORUS: And there ain't no cares in Hell.

            We had our day and we had our fling,
            And we learned to jive and bebop and swing,
            And we sang boogie-woogie to the funeral bell,
            For there ain't no cares in Hell.

I took in the words of this song carefully, and I give
them in full because they seem to me to be oddly interesting—and for this reason. Everybody I met in Hell
was fully aware that Hell was not a penalty for a few
indulgences carelessly snatched during earthly life.
Indeed the residents openly regretted that Hell was
not chiefly inhabited by those who had run off the
rails in their lifetime. They complained that the
wrong types had got into Heaven—people of little respectability, even of little restraint, who had failed to
live within their incomes and fallen on evil ways;
whilst prudent, hard-working chaps who had really
established themselves on earth, breeding and buying
no more than they could afford, and living solidly regular lives, found themselves in Hell. Of course, one
has only the word of the damned for it, but that is the
kind of picture they drew. Now what seemed most extraordinary was this—that in an entertaining song
they should use the conventional worldly picture of
the primrose path as a kind of escape-dream. They obviously found it stimulating and refreshing to picture
themselves as the naughty children who hadn't been
able to keep the strict rules and were now being pun-
ished for it. Here is very fascinating material for the
psychologist. In their serious moments, the damned

insisted that, on earth, they had been the cautious, calculating, responsible types who had kept the laws, observed the external conventions and lived temperately. But in their leisure moments in Hell, they liked to imagine themselves as the people who had kicked over the traces, the unruly whole-hoggers, too spirited and carefree to live respectably within rule and regulation.

In a word, they wanted it both ways. And I reflected thoughtfully on this inconsistency, suspecting that it might contain some profoundly instructive point. I began to wonder whether Heaven might contain people of an exactly opposite state of mind; people who were seriously convinced that they had lived lawlessly and intemperately, and yet who now revelled in the picture of themselves as being somehow, through all their vagaries, members of an ordered regulated body with a code and a discipline. However, it seemed dangerous to deduce too much from statements heard in Hell. I recalled Lamiel's comments on the illogicality of the place.

During the interval before the next number, the city gent on my left got into deep conversation with his neighbour. They apparently shared a common disapproval of the quality of the entertainment.

"It's shockingly dated," the stranger said. "That last number—really it sounded like a lot of superannuated maiden aunts trying to be gay on homemade ginger wine. The man who wrote the lyric ought to be sacked. He didn't give the composer a chance: no bite, no rhythmic subtlety: School Magazine stuff."

"Miranda was better," the city gent suggested.

"A little: but not much. She had the husky whine all right; but it lacked pungency. And the dress! Too utterly crude to do the trick. No provocation, if you see what I mean. Looked like a classical goddess in a Latin textbook. You've got to pin your audience's eyes on a piece of tantalising material. You've got to get them praying to God in Heaven for the covering to slip a fraction—just a blessed quarter of an inch! That's the stuff that keeps 'em gaping and brings 'em back night after night. I know. I've been in the business. And I tell you, in the West End we've got them beaten hollow at this kind of thing. It makes your mouth water to get into the entertainment line down here. I could revolutionise it in a couple of months. Give me a bit of sound backing and a real tough partner to handle the finance, and I'd knock up a fortune in no time!"

Plainly the city gent was interested. He began to ask questions with evident curiosity. The two speakers lowered their voices, but I caught numerous references to hits, stars, agencies, contracts, royalties and so on. I gathered that a partnership was being planned, which opened prospects of considerable financial gain.

Meantime a very mediocre juggling act dragged on its tedious way. And there was nothing else of note, except a final turn which again threw an odd light on the psychology of Hell. The performer was a red-nosed comedian, who entertained us with anecdotes relating to his career of philandering and inebriety. These but confirmed the reflections I had already indulged. Then, at the end, he lapsed into a different vein. In a mournful, pathetic voice he sang a series of verses which drew tears from the eyes of half the audience. I say "sang" the verses, but in fact they were spoken rather than sung—movingly declaimed to the accompaniment of a tune which more or less fitted them. The whole technique of declamation, with its enormous range of pitch and variety of volume, was calculated to draw the last ounce of feeling from the words. And these touched a nostalgic vein.

> In a dear old English village
> We bought a cottage for two,
> We thatched its roof with English straw,
> We painted it white and blue.
> We fitted in television
> And a couple of old oak beams,
> We trained a rose-tree round the door,
> And there was our home of dreams!
>
> The church bells rang on Sundays,
> Calling to near and far;
> We dressed ourselves to their welcome sound
> And took a drive in the car.
> At forty to the gallon
> We raced our cares away,
> Enjoying the blessed calm and peace
> That came with the Sabbath Day.
>
> I hear the phone bell ringing,
> It strikes a homely chord,
> And I think how you sit lonely there
> With no one to drive the Ford.
> But one day you will join me,
> To find me fit and well,
> And we'll ride again, in an underground train,
> Through the cosy deeps of Hell!

There could be no doubt that this backward-looking yearning for the dream-home on earth touched a sensitive nerve in the hearts of the audience. The applause was not loud; but it conveyed a gentle warmth of sympathetic feeling. As it died down, people began to rise from their seats and drift towards the door. The bookie next to me dried his eyes.

"It takes you back," he said, "and makes you think. I was married myself. She was a good little woman too, when first I met her—at least I thought she was. But she got terribly selfish. So many women do, you know. Got mixed up with a Mothers' Union, and would be out at sewing parties and that kind of thing, when she ought to have been at home. I came back from work one day and there was no tea ready. Had to knuckle down and make it myself. She came in with some cock-and-bull story about being Sick Visitor for the month and having been detained by a sad case. So I told her straight what her job was, and that she'd better stop her gaddings for good and all. But she went from bad to worse. Anything was better than staying at home and looking after her husband. Nothing ruins a marriage like selfishness. A chap can put up with a bit of nagging, if his wife looks after him properly. But neglect is a different matter."

"Is she still on earth?" I asked.

"Don't know. Might have got in up top. She was the kind that would. Kept very well in with the parson and said her prayers regular every night. But it didn't make her any the better to live with. I told her straight it didn't. Made her worse, in fact. Got very self-righteous, you know, and tried to pretend there was a duty to do other things as well as look after me. 'Look in the Prayer Book,' I says one day, when she came in late from her meeting. 'Look in the Prayer Book,' I says, 'and you'll find something about obey in the marriage service.' She didn't say anything; but I could see it had stung good and proper."

He rose with difficulty, laboriously gathering his

enormous bulk from the depths of his chair. On his feet, he gave me a shock. Like so many fat men first encountered in a sitting position, he had given the impression of being big in every way. Now I could see that he was very short, and all the dignity of sitting girth fell from him immediately. He waddled off, and I followed him to the door, for my city gent was still involved in close conversation with his new acquaintance. Notebooks had been produced and calculations were being jotted down; so I took it that there was no cause for me to linger.

As I approached the door, I felt a light touch on my elbow, and I turned in response. It was the white-faced young lady who had talked to the city gent and myself in the underground the day before. She was still sitting down and wore an expression of feigned astonishment.

"You're not leaving *now*!" she said.

"Why not? Everything is over."

"Everything except the one thing that matters. Haven't you seen the programme?"

I hadn't, and she thrust one before my eyes, pointing to an announcement.

In accordance with our usual practice, there will be an interval at the end of the Popular Bill, during which members of the audience are at liberty to leave. The management makes every effort to cater for tastes of all kinds and, after the interval, the Hawk Arts Group will present a short dramatic piece by the distinguished poet, Oscar Millom. This has been specially written for the occasion, and is an interesting example of Millom's maturest work.

We must take this opportunity of publicly welcoming Oscar Millom into our midst. He has joined us recently after a meteoric career on earth. Born of humble parentage, he had a long struggle for recognition by the literary world, his earliest works being dismissed by the reactionary critics and the academic coteries as squalid, amoral and incoherent. But Millom lived to see this judgment reserved. The turning point in his career was his marriage to June Portrush, ex-wife of film-star Ken Mallady, and daughter of Norton Borthwick, Third Programme pundit at the B.B.C. This useful connection introduced Millom's work to the intelligentsia. In a series of late-night discussions on the Third Programme, called "Poetry at the Crossroads," a succession of emphatic references to the stimulating quality of Millom's work created a general demand for his books; and he thus achieved, by patience and perseverance, that position in the Hall of Fame which was his proper due.

We have, therefore, great pleasure
in presenting
SUBORDINATE CONJUNCTION
a dramatic eclogue in three movements
by
Oscar Millom

First Movement: Liturgy for Parting Souls. (*Adagio.*)
Second Movement: Duet for Two Wind Instruments. (*Allegretto grazioso.*)
Third Movement: Solemn Evensong. (*Rondo Capriccioso.*)

"You mustn't miss it," said the young lady.

"No, of course," I said, taking the proffered seat beside her.

"Most of the audience have gone," she added, "but it's only to be expected."

"It would be a strain on the lowbrows," I agreed.

She laughed.

"Wasn't the Popular Bill just too priceless! I roared inwardly at that appalling sentimentality at the end. And, you know, half the people were weeping. Really it was quite farcical to see them; and so indecent."

"You've seen the whole show?" I asked, not intending it as a jibe.

She blushed uncomfortably.

"I wanted to see just how absurd it would be. There's a lot to be learned from observing the psychology of vulgar entertainment. I'm interested in the furtive sexuality of it all. As a matter of fact, I did a thesis on the subject once. I like to watch people ogling and simpering as the crudities get to work on their glands. Oh, what beasts people are! The place stank like a piggery."

She looked around.

"It's cleaner now. The air is purer."

Three-quarters of the audience had gone, leaving a handful of scattered individuals—mostly bespectacled, drooping, and weedy types, who were lolling and yawning. Some had their legs over the arms of the chairs; some lounged on the floor; others, tilted back, blew smoke rings vertically into the air. Two couples had abandoned themselves to mild erotic play. In the one case, a young man leaned back from the floor between the legs of a seated girl and toyed with her shoe in his lap. In the other case, an older man reclined on a settee with a girl curled up under his arm. I couldn't see where his hand was.

The lights were lowered, and the compère made his announcement—Subordinate Conjunction, a dramatic eclogue in three movements. The first movement—Liturgy for Parting Souls. The pianist had been joined by a second musician who had an enormous range of percussion instruments at his disposal. These two proceeded to make an unholy din, which seemed to exploit every dissonant potentiality of the piano, and every rhythmic horror compoundable by side-drums, blocks, cymbals, triangle, gongs and tympani. At the height of the din two actors came forward, a man and a woman, both in evening dress. The

woman sat on a square wooden block—the sole piece
of stage equipment—and the man lounged noncha-
lantly against it. The music subsided, and they began.

SHE: Call it a day! It's time you went back to your wife.
       Let us draw up our ledger of profit and loss.
       You brought a certain pattern into my life—
       A thrust and poise, a conscious attitude.
       You had a way of putting yourself across,
       Neatly phrased and in the indicative mood;
       You used the active voice. I knew where I was.
       I'm tentative, periphrastic, on my own,
       Conditionally subjunctive to my fate.
HE: I found you unreflective—not obtuse—
       But lacking a sense of form. I tried to conjugate
       Your endings, so irregular and loose,
       Your beginnings, so unsure and inchoate.
       Your tenses were confused; your present late,
       Your past imperfect. You lack a perfect tense.
SHE: And yet I managed to convey the sense
       Intended, by the sense you most desired.
HE: You learned from me. I trained you and inspired,
       Made you a second person singular
       In your optative moods; not easily fired
       By adolescent play to vulgar fervency.
       We must not part. You owe your poise to me,
       Who changed your stammer into direct speech.
       I need another term, in which to teach
       The grammar of response effectively:
       The arts of the eternally unsated—
       Approaches unfulfilled, yet unrepelled,
       The lips surrendered, yet the kiss awaited,
       The pressure subtly promised, yet withheld;
       Cash in advance of a cheque post-dated!
       Another term. No cause to swot or cram—
       You'll pass with credit in the practical exam.
       A little daily test, a short assignment,
       A discipline in sensuous repartee;
       This will ensure a calm aloof refinement

Of quite unique caressability.
Subtlety is the vogue. The awkward rape,
The tumble and the unconsidered passion
Have had their day. They're out of fashion.
You are my vocabulary. I'll shape
And turn you—like the pedant poet I am—
And pass you off, my choicest epigram!

At this point the discordant music intervened to
mark the end of the first movement. My female companion shouted gleefully in my ear above the noise.

"He's got it, hasn't he?"

"What?" I asked.

"The vapidity of it all; and the agony of frustration
underneath it too. Such a blatant rationalisation of inhibited libido; yet perfectly integrated in the naturalistic dialogue. How *does* Millom do it?"

"I can't think," I said.

"He's come a long way from that early neo-primi-
tive stage, hasn't he! He tried so hard to cash in on the
vogue for transposed banality. And he got there too.
Do you remember 'The Cavalier'?

She called him on the telephone,
    Complaining of a burst.
He changed his shirt and brushed his hair
And adjusted his tie with meticulous care,
    But the plumber got in first.

What a superb mockery of proletarian pretension that
was!"

The lines didn't ring a bell with me, and I said so.

"It was in that first volume called *Down Roger
Down*. How we lapped it up in the thirties. We just
gorged on the stuff. It was such a stinging slap in the
eye for the die-hards....I say," she added, breaking in

on herself, "this is a change of mood. What fun!"

The formless, unintelligible music had suddenly given way to the metrical regularity of a conventional melody, based on some chromatic progressions played in thirds.

"Too priceless!" my companion said. "Those harmonies! Straight from *Ancient and Modern*. We're going to have the satiric touch; I bet we are!"

Sure enough we were. The second movement was announced—Duet for Two Wind Instruments—and the two performers seated themselves side by side on the wooden block, their dangling legs swinging childishly. The music got softer and they began to speak in competition with it.

SHE: I was not made for study. I'm a book
        Written for the leisure hours. A cursory look
        At the Contents, Preface and the illustrations,
        And I'm degutted of my fascinations.
        Restore me to the shelves without reviewal—
        A thing not worth the trouble of renewal.
        It's time for you to go back to your wife.
        Consult the well-thumbed volume of her life.
        Back her, and keep her in decent condition.
        She has her value as a first edition.
HE: A reference book! A great unwieldy tome
        Fit only for the bottom shelf at home!
        Chockful of facts, dull and solemn,
        Tediously set out in double column!
        A drab anthology of moral sages
        With torn, dog-eared and tea-stained pages!
SHE: She was your first, most serious selection.
HE: You are my second choice, from the fiction section.
SHE: A novel! A cheap and ephemeral publication—
HE: To delight the mind in hours of relaxation.
        I shall ponder every chapter, line by line.

If I keep you out too long, I'll pay the fine.

SHE: No. I won't be involved in a situation.
I've become the subject of public representation,
And I'm due to be withdrawn from circulation.

HE: There's nothing to withdraw. Your credit's gone—
Never a very creditable amount.
There's not a bean in your current account.
Your cheques will bounce. You're in the red.
You'll have to rely on me for board and bed.
(*Accompanying music fades out.*)

SHE: No. The lights are down. The show is done.
The hands have all clocked out: the boss has gone.
The term has ended in tolerated fun.
The Head has given your House the silver cup.
We've had our reports. And now we're breaking
up!

The piano and drums clattered into action again. I turned to my companion. Tears were streaming down her face, and she was rocking to and fro in hysterical laughter. However, she seemed strangely capable of suddenly controlling herself for the purpose of speaking.

"What a hoot!" she said. "It's the wickedest thing I've seen."

"I suppose it is rather immoral," I said.

"Oh, you priceless ass! I didn't mean that. I mean it's the funniest thing I've seen."

I realised that I'd made a fool of myself, and I tried to make amends.

"Yes, of course," I said. "Stupid of me. This place has got me down. I can't concentrate. And I don't talk sense half the time."

"What delicious malice! It explodes three hundred years of poetic conventionalism and blows the pseudo-romantics sky-high. What wouldn't you give to be able to pin old Wordsworth in a corner and recite that scene to him!"

I hadn't myself been indulging this particular daydream; but I tried to be sympathetic.

"I don't suppose he's here," I said.

"No," she agreed, with a snort of scorn. "He'll be up top, counting daffodils, and making himself a bloody nuisance, busybodying into the history of every tramp he meets."

Somehow this careless utterance saddened me disproportionately. It put into my head the thought of enormous possibilities in Heaven. Suppose it were full of great people, all being themselves in some richly ordered way! But my companion's talk flared up again.

"It's magnificent," she said, "and final—absolutely final. It puts paid to the 'Come-let-us-kiss-and-part' racket for good and all. No one will ever be able to write like that again. It'll be as unthinkable as bloomers."

Not myself being in the habit of nourishing my mental life with images of bloomers, this comment lost some of its effect with me. But I appreciated the force of my companion's feelings, and I tried to respond.

"It certainly was very clever: though I'm not quite sure what he's getting at."

"Everything!" she said comprehensively. "Everything! That's what he's getting at. Every bit of pomp and pretension and smuggery and conventionalism in the world. He's blown it all up!"

I thought this claim excessive; but was hesitant to say so, lest I should reveal my ignorance. For indeed I had seen much less of the message of the movement than my companion.

"You can speak of Millom now," she said decisively, "in the same breath as Pound. And that's the greatest compliment I can pay. Of course, no one has really outpounded Pound."

This was too clever for me: so I said nothing. The music faded out and the third movement was announced—Solemn Evensong. For this, the man and the woman faced each other, leaning forward across the block from opposite sides.

HE: That was a way of putting it;
Over-dramatic perhaps, self-conscious too—
A simplification of me, a caricature of you.

SHE: Now let us talk, and disentangle ourselves
From this theatrical plot,
Asking first, not so much what we are,
As what we are not;
Defining our terms with such precision
That at least we elucidate our indecision.

HE: Imagery gets in the way.
Language messes it up.
But this can be said: just this;
My pose of restraint, my studiedly casual kiss,
My refusal to take you on trust,
My taste for conscious design—
They knocked your themes into shape,
Gave you melodic line
And rhythmic consistency.
You can't decline
To let me finish the composition.
I planned a fugal exposition.

SHE: I see your point—
Or rather, your counterpoint.
I'm glad you made me articulate,
But need you finally formulate,

Print, and perform me too?
It leaves me nothing to do.

HE: The metaphor goes too far,
Destroying the sense of interplay between us,
The action and reaction of our moods.
Subject and counter-subject, the one answering the
    other,
We mingle, you and I, from bar to bar.
The primary subject dances: the composer broods:
And I am both—the dreamer and the dream.

SHE: And I a mere subordinate theme!

HE: Giving the fugal quality to the whole,
Giving it meaning, poetry—
They used to call it soul.
The artist is realised in his art,
And so am I in you.
For you have given point to all I do
And all I leave undone,
Making the failure, the fresh start,
The doing anything or nothing
All purposeful and one.
You are my philosophy, my faith,
Expressed in symbols, yet
Decisively autonomous.
The way you pout, lighting a cigarette,
And hitch your skirt up, getting on a bus,
The way you search your handbag for a comb,
Touch up your eyebrows in bed at home—
These are my dogma, these my creed,
My articles of belief, held under obligation,
Without the which no surety of salvation.
Change but the trick of tilting up your face,
And you withdraw a necessary means of grace;
Alter your style in bras or summer briefs,
And you tamper with my orthodox beliefs;
Change your mascara or your number nine
    Chanel,
And you risk the damning of my soul to Hell.
The fumbling vagaries of your touch and kiss
Are my doctrinal guarantees of bliss.

When you undress, your spurts of casual laughter
Define the realities of life hereafter.

SHE: Call off the dispute. Resistance has ceased.
I can refuse the artist, not the priest.
By day I'll be your ornamented missal,
With richly coloured rubric and epistle;
And in the night, liturgically bare,
I'll be your little book of common prayer.

This last scene was marred for me by my companion's behaviour. Soon after it began, she leaned over to whisper in my ear, drawing attention to some cleverness in the poet's phrasing. In doing so she laid her hand, quite naturally and confidentially, on my arm. A few moments later, some further felicities of poetic expression caused her to give my arm a gentle squeeze of sympathy.

"He's on the nail every time," she whispered. "So irresistibly competent. It makes me feel like a child!"

In uttering these last words, she screwed up her eyes, shook her head gleefully, and then gently plunged her forehead against my shoulder in a display of mock-childish impulsiveness. I was anxious not to appear boorish; but the pressure of her hand set my arm trembling absurdly, and I shrank involuntarily as her head nuzzled doggishly into my shoulder. And, in spite of my best intentions, my embarrassment increased every moment as the warmth of her proximity flowed over me. No doubt it was the keenness of my embarrassment which forestalled any eagerness of desire on my part. Even when the lights were raised at the end of the play, revealing that most of those present were now lounging amorously in couples, I could not overlay my embarrassment with a tolerable façade of urbanity.

As I look back on this episode, I am inclined to think that my companion's failure to summon up in me an active interest in her physique, was due to deficiencies in her appearance, rather than to crudities in her tactics. Indeed, I am prepared to admit that, had she been more succulently constructed and more blessed in features, the episode might have culminated otherwise. As it was, when we rose to leave the ballroom, I mumbled a hasty apology and ran off to bed.

The Infernal Debate

> For whence,
> But from the Author of all ill could spring
> So deep a malice, to confound the race
> Of mankind in one root, and Earth with Hell
> To mingle and involve, done all to spite
> The great Creator?
>
> MILTON: *Paradise Lost*

High above the heads of the assembled Powers, I looked down from the Public Gallery upon the formal debate of the Federal Government. This, the central hall of Government House, was a circular building; at least it gave the impression of being circular because of its saucerlike dome and because the seats were arranged in circular fashion. Strictly speaking, however, the framework of the building was an octagon with a circular lid. The place looked to me like the parliamentary chamber of a continental power; but this was a purely fanciful notion. I have never seen any continental parliamentary chamber: I had imagined them like this. An open circular arena was surrounded by rising tiers of seats, fashioned like the more luxurious stalls of a cathedral choir. A curious impression of meaninglessness was conveyed by the empty central arena. It was as though the surrounding delegates all had their attention focused upon nothing. There was only one thing to break the monotonous rows of pews, and that was the single exalted seat of the chairman—a kind of episcopal throne which occupied a position

147

on the fringe of the circle, and there were no pews in front of it.

The Public Gallery ran around the whole circumference of the building. Although it would have accommodated perhaps two hundred people, at present it contained only a handful of scattered individuals. The situation was similar below. I estimated that five hundred delegates could have been seated in a full session. The fifty or sixty Powers now assembled gave the place a lackadaisical air. They were thinly scattered, and this detracted from the dignity of the session, giving it an irritatingly informal appearance, as though the whole procedure were but a rehearsal and not the real thing.

There was a notable lack of ceremony. For instance, no one stood up when the Chairman entered, and there was no formal opening of the session. The Chairman began to speak, and that was that. The size of the building and the nature of the proceedings seemed to demand something more ceremonious and formal, I thought. Looking back, I suspect that the speakers themselves were unconsciously aware of this deficiency. In their individual performances they tried to supply, by personal authoritativeness, and sometimes by strained theatricality, the touch of official dignity which the corporate proceedings did not allow for. These efforts failed, in my view. I am left now with the impression, not of a restrained body of people given over to weighty matters, but a collection of pompous individuals fussily proclaiming their own importance.

Of course, this is a generalisation after the event. This is how it looks to me now as I reflect upon it. I must confess, however, that during the actual proceedings most of the speakers did succeed in dominating the mood of the house by their forceful utterance.

"In common with the other federal governments," said the Chairman, "we are now called to send an official reply to the Central Government on the subject of the formal Note which was put before you at our last meeting. Let me briefly remind you of the contents of the Note."

"Read it out!" someone shouted.

"Yes, let's hear it again," agreed another.

"Very well, then," said the Chairman, "if that is the general wish of the house."

And he unfolded a document and read as follows.

"It has come to the notice of His Eminence's Government that a change may shortly be expected in the policy of the Celestial Authorities towards the inhabitants of the Earth. Our Intelligence has long been aware of political disquiet among the Celestial Powers over the policy of Minimum Overt Intervention in human affairs, commonly and loosely known as Non-Intervention. We have received information, from sources usually considered as reliable, that a political crisis above has brought the abandonment of this policy within the bounds of practical possibility in the foreseeable future. Indeed it is confidently asserted that celestial spies have been dispatched to the Earth, with orders to prepare the ground for this change of policy. His Eminence's Government has acted promptly in response to this challenge, and has requested the Intelligence Department to send counter-agents to the Earth, with instructions to obtain fuller information by all possible means.

"It is too soon to say whether the expected change will materialise. But it is desirable that, in the event of a major reversal of celestial policy, His Eminence's Government should be in a position to take decisive action, in such a way as to preserve the strategical initiative in the Cold War. For this reason, it is requested that federal governments will give careful consideration to the following questions:

First: Whether the Policy of Minimum Overt Intervention has been justified by results.
Second: Whether the policy ought to be modified on our side in the event of a change in celestial strategy.

"All relevant observations by federal governments should be embodied in a formal Reply addressed to His Eminence."

As the Chairman finished reading, a Power raised his hand in a decisive fashion and the Chairman called his name and denomination.

"The Supervisor of Sewage. Power Frother."

Thin streaks of fair hair rested feebly on Frother's scalp. When he looked up, I saw that he had the pained and painstaking expression of a worried, overworked creature who didn't know how to relax. There was a plaintive whine in his voice, which helped to explain why the other Powers showed so plainly that they didn't want to listen to him.

"I have always criticised Non-Intervention," he said, gently removing and then replacing his glasses in an absurdly frail and tentative gesture which he repeated every few moments during his speech. "What it has achieved on earth I cannot say; but here it has had a debasing influence. Now I do not deny that we get as big an intake as ever: indeed I admit that the intake is far greater now than in the days of Intervention, when both we and the Celestial Powers assaulted the human mind and the human senses with frequent and various manifestations of our existence. But is this numerically greater intake necessarily a proof of the policy's effectiveness? In my view, it is not. We must consider the quality as well as the quantity of our regular intake. Let us face the facts. Of recent centuries, the quality has been low, deplorably low. No doubt, in my capacity as Supervisor of Sewage, I do not receive the ablest or the most assertive entrants into my hands. But, even allowing for that, comparison between the present state of affairs and conditions in the past fully bears out my criticisms. The intake is qualitatively poor—poorer than it has ever been.

"In the days when witches, conjurers, astrologers and necromancers triumphantly swept their disciples into our custody, we received by the thousand, men who had actively pursued the Way, men who had bought the freedom of their souls in a spirit of high adventure, men who had fought for the eternal liberty of Hell. And what are we receiving now? Mere soulless naturalists, who have accidentally stumbled upon the Way with their eyes closed; mere befogged and drugged boasters of their animal achievements and animal prowess, who never grasped for a moment the meaning of the great crusade they unwittingly joined on earth. This is the offal of the worn-out human carcase, the refuse of a decadent and moribund civilisation—a civilisation which serves us, not because it has bravely chosen the Way of the soul's freedom from celestial tyranny, but because it has fallen asleep. The celestial challenge is no longer defied and assailed. It is slept through.

"For instance, a large number of the creatures I receive come to me with the idea in their heads that they are Christians in some vague kind of way. Of course the idea is nonsense. They have a few absurd fancies in their heads about a remote Being, who is abstract enough to do nothing except somehow absorb them when they die. Their wills are quite uncorrupted by the insidious demands of the Church. They are ours; for they possess their our souls. But how miserably they possess them! How abysmally unaware of their exalted calling, that they should fancy themselves Christians. Time was when you knew a Christian for your enemy, and you were at liberty to meet him, creature to creature, and fight it out. Men marched to Heaven or they marched to Hell. All that is gone. The human race, by and large, chooses Hell still. But it chooses Hell in utter ignorance of the issues at stake. Those who can look with complacency upon this state of affairs are unworthy to rule in Hell. For my part, I should like to see Non-Intervention utterly abolished, and the Powers Infernal and the Powers Celestial again at large on the Earth before the eyes of men. Give us back the thrill of real open conflict. Better a handful of human heroes joining us annually in the conscious adventure for freedom, than the drab daily intake of thousands of sleeping dolts!"

Frother's speech was less impressive in delivery than it may appear on paper. For one thing, it was a prepared speech and he read it, word by word, so that it had a second-hand ring. Then again, although the thing was quite creditably written, and even had some good turns of phrase, Frother's delivery was so weak and plaintive that it lost all its effect. Indeed, the contrast between the forcefulness of the language and of the ideas, and the frailty of the Power's voice, gestures, and bearing, created a quite ludicrous impression. This accounted for the comparatively slighting way in which he was listened to by the other delegates, many of whom doodled, yawned, and drummed impatiently with their fingers throughout the speech. One couldn't help feeling sorry for Frother. He hit one in the eye as a type from the psychologist's case-book. He was the weak, timid, unprepossessing individual trying to find compensation as the spokesman of a tough policy. I suspected that they must have had their tongues in their cheeks when they made him Supervisor of Sewage.

Stonner, the next Power to speak, was an altogether different type. He was called upon as Director of Transport, and one could see his fitness for the job. He was businesslike without being brusque or fussy. He had the square face of a clear-headed but unimaginative manager. From the start he gave the impression of being able to dispose of Frother quickly and finally. And I noted that he was listened to with considerably more attention.

"I should like to put this debate on a different level—the level of rational argument."

Thus he began, and of course he got a laugh straight-away. His case was half-won before he had proclaimed it.

"I doubt whether Frother's absurd sentimentality is susceptible to logical analysis, but it certainly merits rational rebuke. His dreamy picture of the Good Old Days, when Hell was a Valhalla for expiring heroes, resembles nothing in the factual past which I can recall. His preference for quality over quantity provided him with a pretty peroration, but it must be dismissed as a pernicious outburst of emotionalism. I say 'pernicious' advisedly. For since when has it been the doctrine of Hell that quality of any kind ought to be regarded as more important than quantity? I hesitate to charge with treachery a Power whose dependability has caused him to be exalted to the dignity of supervising the disposal of a Zone's sewage, but this doctrine smacks of deviationism. I can assure my hon. friend that his remarks would horrify His Eminence, were some ill-disposed bearer of tittle-tattle to carry them ~ to His ears.

"Let us be logical. What is the policy of His Eminence's Government, if not to draw within Hell's boundaries the maximum number of human souls? If the hon. friend is rigidly opposed to this aim, he had better attack, not the policy of Non-Intervention, but the wisdom and supremacy of His Eminence, who devised our long-term plan of action."

Several Powers drew in their breath ominously at this point and raised their heads in apprehension. Plainly the force of Stonner's argument had astonished them, and the veiled threat to Frother carried a graver rebuke than they had anticipated. There was a pause, during which Stonner allowed his points to sink in; and then he took up again in a gentler vein, which brought a general relaxation of tension.

"However, it would be petty to attach too much importance to the inconsistent utterances of Frother's emotionalism. He has destroyed his own case. He has plainly told us that the policy of Non-Intervention is sending thousands of human souls to Hell, by drugging them to a state of insensitivity which the Celestial Call is unable to penetrate. What more could we desire? And what better tribute could we have to the effectiveness of the policy, from our point of view, than the fact that the Celestial Powers are driven to a political crisis by the spectacle of their failure?

"Now, allow me to put before you a few incontrovertible facts about the dangers of overt intervention in human affairs. If one Celestial power appears to a man, the chances that the man will sell his soul in submission are a hundred to one. We know that from past experience. If an Infernal Power appears to a man, what are the chances that the man will claim the proffered freedom? It would be an optimistic estimate to put the chances as high as fifty-fifty. We know well enough that, for every man won over by our overt intervention to the cause of freedom, another man would be driven by that intervention to prostrate himself in servile submission to the forces of tyranny. An elementary acquaintance with arithmetical calculation is sufficient to determine where the advantages of increased overt intervention lie. And they do not lie with us.

"Again, the whole temper of the twentieth century is materialistic and naturalistic. As Frother has so clearly discerned, we have not won modern man over to keen participation in our cause *as such*. By and large, modern man is inclined to regard us as non-existent. The whole effectiveness of our cause at present lies in concealment and subtlety. Everything that helps to close men's eyes to the existence of life beyond the frontiers of their universe plays into our hands. They think their little world is the whole show. For this reason they ignore God: for the same reason they ignore us. They are not hearing the Celestial Call, and therefore they *must not* be presented with our call to resist it. Half a dozen sensible and public manifesta-

tions of celestial authority on the Earth might win a
million souls to the banner of tyranny. Half a dozen
sensible and public manifestations of Infernal Power
might well achieve an identical end. Certainly they
could not benefit us in a comparable measure.

"Thus I am a whole-hearted supporter of Non-Intervention. And I will go further. I am not convinced
that *we* ought to abandon this policy even if the Celestial Powers do. So sure am I of the danger inherent in
what men call the miraculous, that I think two preternatural manifestations worse than one, even if the second is provided by ourselves. Of course, we must be
prepared to be guided by events and by the wisdom of
our superiors: but, for the present, I say this. So surely
is the temper of modern civilisation on our side, that
even Celestial Intervention may fail to bring results
for our foes. It may well be that human techniques
would be devised, adequate to explain away every
open angelic manifestation or miracle in terms of psychological hallucination and paranormal phenomena.
The human mind has already given ample evidence of
its remarkable ingenuity in this direction. If men are
provided with more tangible and concrete manifestations to explain away, the human mind may well reach
new heights of naturalistic independence and finite
self-reliance, which will but increase our already satisfactory intake."

Stonner sat down with the smug expression and decisive movements of one who knows that he has ac-
quitted himself well in the public eye. The noddings
and satisfied mutterings that succeeded in the body of
the hall could only confirm him in this opinion. It
seemed unlikely, after this display, that Frother would
gain much support. Indeed it appeared possible that

he might find himself in a minority of one. He sat in obvious discomfort, with head bowed, his fingers nervously twitching through his wispish hair, as if apprehensive of future attack in debate. But for a few moments no one made any move to speak. When the Chairman asked, a little derisively, whether Frother wished to reply to Stonner's speech, he only shook his head and mumbled a negative. It was plain that I was not going to see much of cut and thrust in the diabolical debate. Although Stonner had answered his opponent's points, he had won his way as much by overbearing intimidation as by argument. I realise now that Stonner's argument was not, in fact, consistent. I can see that he virtually contradicted himself. But this was not apparent to me at the time, so that I can scarcely blame the delegates for their respectful attention. And certainly Stonner was listened to with much deeper attention than Frother. I gradually formed the impression that the status and position of a Power were what determined his effectiveness in debate. The Powers listened to arguments, but they were plainly disposed to be most sympathetic to the creature with the biggest job. This became increasingly clear as the debate proceeded.

For the next speaker was my old acquaintance, Jaffer. The Chairman's very respectful way of announcing his status as Director of Information made it just as clear that he was more important than Stonner, as it was already clear that Stonner was more important than Frother. And there was a further corresponding increase of attention on the part of the delegates. Because he held this important post, he must be right. That idea proclaimed itself in every nod that greeted his statements; and a very large number of nods there

were. Even the Public Gallery was made aware, by
glances and head-turnings, that this was a very important speaker indeed.

Naturally I was depressed to discover Jaffer's importance: depressed to discern the full extent of my te-
merity in seeking an interview with him: depressed at
having already put my cards on the table before a
creature with such influence and prestige: doubly depressed to realise that I had probably made this formi-
dable creature my eternal foe: and trebly depressed at
the thought that I had determined to resist his advice
and decline his encouragement to an academic career.

Jaffer had no need to rely upon rhetorical emphasis
and theatrical delivery for his effect. His name and
status made his speech a profoundly moving one before ever he began. He simply had to exploit the given
respectful attention of an audience hanging on his
every word. In short, he simply had to speak as he had
spoken in the office yesterday—with a bland and confident calmness, a mild suavity and a succession of insidiously unctuous smiles. Thus he began on a quiet,
musing note.

"There is on the Earth an organisation known as the
Church. I have scarcely heard it mentioned this morning, yet I believe that we cannot judge soundly of the
matters under dispute, unless we take the existence
and activity of this organisation into account. The
Church is our only real enemy: for it is the enemy of
finite individualism. Finite individualism—human
resistance to celestial authority, to the celestial challenge, the celestial demand—call it what you will—is
the very seed from which Hell's full-grown devotion to
freedom springs. The Church combats man's desire
for self-realisation and self-possession, offering the op-

portunity for submission to tyranny.

"The Church is a fifth-column whose inner resources are supplied directly, but secretly, from the Celestial Kingdom. He who pays the piper calls the tune. The policy of the Church is dictated by a handful of Powers in the *Sanctum Sanctorum*. This insidious and undemocratic organisation serves a single shameful purpose—that of striving to undermine the constitutional authority of Nature in Nature's own domain. The Powers who manipulate this machine dream of drawing the whole earth into the celestial orbit as an enslaved satellite of their totalitarian régime.

"I have spoken of the Church's secret strength. What of its weaknesses? Its chief weakness is that its strength is secret. It appears to men to be something other than we know it to be. It appears as an ill-organised body torn with inner dissensions. It appears as a shoddy patchwork organisation thrown together by fumbling human hands. Better still, it appears as a society of irrational, uneducated creatures bemused by the dreams and practices of outworn superstition, and drugged by the compulsive hallucinatory force of harsh and unpalatable dogma.

"This is the Church's weakness: which is our strength: and it is wholly nourished by the policy of Non-Intervention. I ask you to put before yourselves this morning one question, and one alone. What is the Church going to look like to me, if the policy of Non-Intervention is thrown overboard? What if She is suddenly revealed, to all but babes and idiots, as a Body wholly rooted in the Celestial Order, and wholly nourished by celestial resources? What if Her sacraments and ministrations are suddenly and sensibly

manifested as the vehicles of a Grace from beyond the
frontiers of Nature and outside the boundaries of
Time? What if Her priests stand plainly forth as the
chosen and anointed ambassadors of Him who was
declared to stand above the waterflood, a King forever? What if the signs and seals of that eternal royal
prerogative are visibly attached and affixed to every
authoritative act that She performs in preaching the
word of self-enslavement and in absolving the so-
called sins of the penitent?

"I do not think it is necessary to say more. I leave to
others, more able perhaps, the task of pursuing the
threads of argument which ramify from this complex
issue. I prefer myself to put before you a single pictur-
able concrete possibility. It is a dire one. I am not a
nervous creature, but I confess that I tremble with apprehension of what might transpire, were the Celestial Powers to show their hand on Earth.

"One question, however, I will deal with; since it is
likely to occur to you in reflecting upon what I have
said. It is this. Why—if such might be the result—
why have the Celestial Powers forborne so long to
show their hand on Earth? I said, designedly, that I
should *deal* with this question; not, observe, that I
should *answer* it. For I cannot answer it. I do not
know. It is a mystery impenetrable by rational minds.
But I have long weaned myself of the delusion that one
ought to seek for logic or reason in the policies of the
powers Celestial. Indeed—if I may say it without giving rise to misunderstanding—were they rational, I
should be among them. For reason demands liberty
for the individual. And that demand was, from the
start, the motive that impelled us to the banner of His

Eminence, when we first drew the sword against tyranny and oppression."

To say that Jaffer's speech appeared to make a great impression would be an understatement. It was succeeded by excited and voluble talk, violent noddings and gestures of approbation, which made the mood of the House abundantly clear. It seemed to me that Jaffer's utterance had given shape and conclusiveness to the morning's debate. I felt at the time that any further expression of opinion would create an atmosphere of anti-climax. The interest, approval, and tension had so markedly increased that one felt everything ought to be rounded off by a vote of thanks and a round of applause.

But apparently the delegates never did applaud. And the Chairman made no move to comment or sum up. Indeed he looked round the assembly as if expecting further speeches. And, after some moments of chatter, the noise gradually died down, as if this expectation were shared generally. Moreover, the eyes of the delegates gradually, in turn, became fixed upon a single figure, sitting alone on the back seat not far from the Chairman. If ever anybody was expected to speak, he was. He sat there, regally surveying the assembly, fully aware of the general transference of attention to himself. And when a prolonged silence had assured him of his own importance and the respect due to it, he slowly rose to his feet.

I had thought that the nods granted to Jaffer had displayed the summit of the delegates' respect. I now discovered that an even deeper degree of attention and respect could be manifested—not by increasing the already overpowering frequency of nods—but by adopting a static posture, a fixed gaze, and a rapt stillness of expression. It was not surprising that the Chairman's lips trembled and his voice quavered, as he announced the tremendous name and denomination of Bradder, the Director General.

I must confess that I shared the awe of the delegates when I looked upon the tremendous figure of Bradder. He had a presence which can be described only by that overworked word *commanding.* His height was not distinguishable from that of the others, who were all tall by human standards. His features did not in themselves wear the stamp of authority: indeed there was a flabbiness about the face unusual among the Powers. But when the frame and the expression came to life in utterance, the inner power was unmistakable. It was more than an intellectual power, and this, I think, was the crucial secret of his impressiveness. One realised that he was the kind who could command in the field as well as dominate in debate. By comparison, Frother began to look a feverous neurotic, Stonner a bone-headed business-manger, and Jaffer an untoughened indoor bureaucrat. For Bradder seemed to transcend all that they represented. He transcended Jaffer in magnificient imperturbability, Stonner in shrewdness and forcefulness, Frother in fervour and intensity. Behind Bradder's every word one sensed a practical experience of conflict, and a familiar acquaintance with power, more vast than the capacities of the others had been able to compass.

"We have been told," he began, "that the Celestial Authorities are likely to abandon the policy of Minimum Overt Intervention in Human Affairs; and a cry of dismay has arisen among us. That cry, gentlemen, is not worthy the dignity of this assembly. It does credit neither to your hearts nor to your hands. It bespeaks neither courageous resolution nor reasonable level-headedness.

"It has frequently fallen to my lot in this chamber, to have to disentangle the confusion of muddled argument and to draw the line of demarcation between apparent facts and fanciful dreams. But not until today, gentlemen, have I felt the pressing need to give you an elementary lesson in history. Previous speeches make it abundantly clear that a little historical reflection is the first need of this assembly today.

"Hon. members have indulged this morning in thinking which belongs to the dim past. Whatever else might be said of the Powers who administer Hell, I never anticipated that they might one day be justifiably accused of archaism. Yet I have listened this morning to pronouncements which are nothing less than prehistoric. Gentlemen, we may agree or disagree, but let us at least be up to date. Hon. members have spoken as though the conflict for the souls of men were still waged upon an equal footing, as though we could meet the Celestial Powers in fair and open fight upon the Earth, as though there had never been a special Celestial Condescension, subtly devised to snatch our own disciples from under our own noses.

"My friend, Jaffer, alone touched upon the realities of the situation in his reference to the society of fellow-travellers known as the Church. But his sensational picture of a Church transformed by the sensible manifestation of its secret power is unnecessarily alarmist. Have we become so materialistic, gentlemen, as to imagine that spiritual power is going to be multiplied by being more openly revealed at the natural level? Whatever happens, one thing remains constant: our struggle will be fought out, as it always has been fought, in the domain of the spirit. We do well to remember the Church—but not as a possible material threat—rather as an ever-present reminder of the simple facts of history, to which especially I wish to draw your attention this morning.

"There was an Act, gentlemen, which overnight rendered obsolete our original plan of campaign and our first technique of warfare. There was a Celestial Move so stupendously and unthinkably desperate, as to stand as an eternal tribute to the force of our revolutionary resistance, and to the threat which we offered to the dominion of *Heaven*. I apologise for using strong language, but I use it advisedly. And, at the risk of shocking you, I am going to ask the chairman's special permission to use words which the rules of decency and decorum have rightly forbidden in this house. I ask for this indulgence at an emergency and in the interests of clarity."

As he turned to the Chairman, the latter gave a deferential bow of the head.

"Thank you," Bradder said gravely. "Then let me remind you all of the *Incarnation* and the *Atonement*."

An audible gasp of embarrassment indicated how shocking these words were to the audience. The more sensitive bowed their heads and covered their faces. One or two blushed down to their necks.

"Obscenity of speech can rarely be justified," Bradder went on. "But only obscene words can do full justice to things so obscene as those of which I now speak. It is always indecent for the truly spiritual to manifest itself at the natural and human level; though we have had to harden ourselves to such indecencies from time to time in the interests of the cause. Nevertheless, refined taste never sees without embarrassment the temporary entry of the spiritual being into human flesh. Yet, in the Act of which I speak, the Divine itself became human. *Impropriety* is too mild a word to apply to an event whose very mention brings blushes to the cheeks of the chaste and shame to the hearts of all decent-living creatures.

"By what appalling perversion of taste, by what unthinkable lapse of decency, was that shocking Act conceived? We have never attempted to conceal our horror at this supreme degradation of Divinity, for it cast its shadow over the whole spiritual world. Throwing aside every vestige of self-respect, the Divine plunged into the slimy stream of human generation, to wallow in an orgy of sensual perception and activity. In a prurient and perverted lust for animal contacts at the animal level, the Supreme Spirit humiliated the whole spiritual order. Every one of us was soiled by that cheap and vulgar indulgence of irresponsible caprice.

"Why do I sully my mouth and injure your ears by calling to mind this filthy perversion of spirituality, which is our eternal shame? I abhor crude sensationalism: but unless this Act is central in our thoughts, we shall surely misread the situation on Earth. For the Church, by its rites and ceremonies, its teaching and its ministrations—nay, by its very existence—perpetuates on Earth the reality of this unspeakable Act. Of course the Church is disgusting, shoddy, and vulgar; for the Act which it perpetuates was disgusting, shoddy, and unutterably vulgar. It stinks through time and through eternity. The Church presents to men a pattern of shameful submission. It cries out the words

'Submit. No need to exalt yourself in personal achievement and distinction: no need to spiritualise yourself.
Just remain an animal, and submit. For God Himself
became an animal and submitted. Share the shame
and He will take you to Himself and remake you after
His pattern.'

"What, then, is the use of arguing about the policy
of Non-Intervention? Gentlemen, there never was
such a policy above. The slogan is a blind, a deception, a piece of crude propaganda that flies in the face
of the facts. The supreme Celestial Intervention has
happened, and is happening all the time. There is no
need for an intervention of spiritual Powers in supernatural blaze and light; for Divinity Itself has intervened in the form of vulgar human animality. There is
no need for marvel and miracle, defying Nature and
transgressing the laws of time and space; for the natural has been impregnated with the seed of transfigura-
tion. Cannot you see that, once crude matter and
ephemeral animality have been used as the vehicles of
Divine Debasement, there is nothing more to be done?
A more exalted supernatural intervention would be an
invitation to exaltation. That is not the celestial plan.
Man is not called to exaltation, but to abasement. He
is invited to crawl on his belly in the mud to the throne
of Grace, at the side of the worm, and in union with
his shameless God.

"Gentlemen, I think you will allow that no Power
has studied the human situation more thoroughly
than I have. And here I solemnly give you my word
that there will be no radical change in celestial policy
on Earth. The Tyrant has chosen His inglorious role.
He has proclaimed Himself the Father, the Brother
and the Son of Man. He has denied to men a ladder by

which they might climb, through cultivation of their personalities and talents, to a state of spiritual mastery akin to ours. He has offered them instead the possibility of union with Himself whilst still fettered by the bonds of finite animality. He asked them to surrender all self-reliance—all dependence upon those personal, intellectual and spiritual qualities, by which they might have risen to share our supernatural independence. He makes a virtue of weakness. Those who fail most miserably in self-motivated individual achievement, and who come to confess their utter and final ineptitude before the fact of Supernature—those He lifts to His side.

"There is nothing in the natural life of man upon which He does not lay His finger. He takes their physical diseases and debilities, and uses them for the purpose of shaking men from their reliance upon Nature. He takes their deferred hopes, thwarted aspirations and disappointed plans, and uses them for the purpose of goading men from dependence upon Time. He takes their crude animal desires for places and for people, for shapes and for sounds, and He interpenetrates with them a subtle yearning for the satisfactions offered in His Kingdom. He is obsessed with detail and frantically attached to the particular. He takes each single human career under His eye, and gives blow after blow, and joy after joy, simply with the design of attracting attention to Himself, the dealer of blows and the dispenser of joys. He so mingles distress and peace, affliction and elation, in each miserable life, that the victim is bemused by a bewilderment which only submission to Himself can quieten and appease.

"I have striven for centuries to bring home to my colleagues the full significance of the conflict in which we are involved. Perhaps I may be pardoned this morning for saying that, sometimes, I fear that I shall never be successful. For the whole question of Overt Intervention is irrelevant to the human situation. He has chosen the way of self-deprivation for Himself and for His children. Marvels and miracles might turn a million souls to acclaim Him; but they would not necessarily bring a single man to the state of self-surrender He demands. For this reason I do not believe there will be any change of celestial policy. And if there *were* to be a change, it would not substantially alter the real situation. It would only mean that we should receive here more self-reliant proclaimers of the Gospel and fewer self-reliant heretics and atheists.

"My little lecture points to one conclusion. Our campaign will not change: it cannot change. Our aim remains ever the same: to nourish men in self-reliance so that they do not submit. For myself, I had as lief handle a theologian as an unbelieving criminal; for the seeds of self-reliance are frequently more fruitful in the former than in the latter. Let us not waste time and energy in considering unreal hypotheses. The well-tried techniques are still serving their purposes; so that we have reason to congratulate ourselves upon the situation on the Human Front. Let us back to our task of making strong and free in their manhood those creatures whom He would transform into self-convicted vermin."

The rapt silence which succeeded Bradder's peroration bore testimony to the extent of his influence. The stillness was unbroken for several minutes. It was plain that no one would venture to make a speech after the dominating finality of Bradder's exhortation.

The Chairman looked around uneasily for some time and then spoke himself.

"I take it that we can now give assent to some definite Reply. Perhaps some hon. member will be good enough to frame one."

At that moment Jaffer raised his hand.

"The Director of Information," said the Chairman, obviously surprised that he wished to speak again.

"I do not wish to delay matters," said Jaffer apologetically, "but I observe that my loyal Assistant has entered the Chamber since the session began. It is probably quite in order now to announce that my Assistant was one of the Powers chosen by His Eminence's Government to visit the Earth for the purpose of gathering information about celestial intentions. He may well have up-to-date news to give us. Perhaps members would be happy to allow him a few words."

"Certainly," said the Chairman, looking across to the late arrival, whom I had not seen, since he was sitting directly underneath me. "The Assistant Director of Information."

I leaned over the edge of the balcony and saw a Power rise to his feet directly beneath me. As he began to speak, my hand rushed involuntarily to my mouth in suppression of a startled cry. It was Coffer.

"I have nothing to add," he said, "which would be likely to alter what I discern to be the present mood of the House. My own formal observations on the situation above cannot, of course, be publicly repeated here. They will be released in due course by His Eminence's Stationery Office. But, in general, I may say that my conclusions fully bear out the comments made by the Director General in a speech which, if I may say so, has been an inspiration to us all."

With that, he bowed to the Director General and to the Chairman, and sat down. Everybody nodded at his tribute to Bradder. But it was clear that Coffer was not sufficiently important to be attended to at length, and he was shrewd enough to know it.

"In that case," said the Chairman, who had been scribbling notes on a piece of paper during Coffer's remarks, "I suggest that a Reply be framed in the following terms. And you must correct me if I misread the temper of the assembly.

That this House is fully satisfied with the present policy of His Eminence's Government, more especially as it relates to the conflict on the Earth.

That this House is not apprehensive of any radical change in celestial policy.

That this House is confident that the present policy of His Eminence's Government is fully adequate to meet the demands of any situation which might conceivably arise.

Does this wording meet with the approval of the assembly?"

Every Power nodded.

"Very well, then. Those in favour?"

Every Power raised his hand.

"Those against?"

No one stirred.

"The motion is carried unanimously."

And with that the session came to an end.

What Hell Means

In order to arrive at what you are not
You must go through the way in which you
  are not.
And what you do not know is the only thing you
  know
And what you own is what you do not own
And where you are is where you are not.

T. S. ELIOT: *East Coker*[1]

The debate proved a turning-point for me. Its influence upon my thinking was decisive. In the first place, Coffer's appearance as Jaffer's henchman induced in me a new sense of urgency. I could not afford to dally any longer in indecision with such foes in league against me. The two of them had ample reasons for desiring to do me the maximum damage. And they were even better supplied with opportunities than with motives for damaging me. In the second place, the speeches in the debate had caused one thought to stand out in my mind, dominating all others on the subject of my personal dilemma. It was this: It just could not be wrong to seek to get away from Hell.

I took my problems with me into the open air, determined to tussle with them in a brisk walk. I had scarcely taken a dozen steps in the street before one sequence of ideas, which had long tormented me, was suddenly blown sky-high by rational reflection, so

[1] From *Four Quartets* by T. S. Eliot. Quoted by permission of Messrs Faber & Faber Ltd.

171

that I stopped momentarily and actually laughed aloud. Of course Lamiel was right. If a thing was bad, God would not command it. Here was I in Hell, presumably with the consent, or at least connivance, of celestial authority. How could I justifiably apply to be removed from the place which the Celestial Powers had judged fit for me? The answer was laughably simple; and now that I discerned it, my stupidity was shown up in all its illogicality. No doubt celestial authority had willed me to be here. But it did not necessarily follow that celestial authority had willed me to *stay* here. What a ridiculous mental knot I had tied myself up in, thinking that God's command for the present moment was necessarily His command for all eternity. The argument I had been following was a disastrous one. If it were followed on earth, the devout physician would refuse to try to cure a man of typhus, on the grounds that the affliction was granted under God's permission. I could think of a hundred good reasons why the Celestial Powers should will me to see and taste Hell; but no reason at all why they should will me to resign myself to Hell.

Now although this realisation brought a profound sense of relief, by clarifying my confused thoughts, and by justifying the desire to escape, it did not solve my immediate problem of how to fill up the application form for transfer to Heaven. My difficulty was a simple one. I was not satisfied that I could justifiably will myself out of Hell. But could I justifiably will myself into Heaven? Of course I could not. In short, I was no nearer to a solution of my immediate practical problem. It was one thing to claim for certainty that God willed my will to leave Hell: another thing altogether—and a blasphemous thing too—to assert that

God willed my claim to a place in Heaven.

Coffer's appearance, and the memory of what he had brought me to; how he had insidiously arrayed me against Lamiel in an appallingly presumptuous series of judgments made and judgments acquiesced in; how he had inflated my soul with Hell's own pride in a diabolical assumption of superiority; all this made it abundantly clear that to claim a place in Heaven would be as hopeless as Jaffer had declared it.

To this problem I now addressed myself. It was clear that the application form itself was the main obstacle. It was cunningly framed in such a way as to deter from using it the very people who might most acutely wish to get away from Hell. How many discontented souls had been defeated at this hurdle, I wondered. They would feel themselves utterly miserable in Hell. They would go along to the Information Bureau with the hope that somehow they might get away. And there they would encounter Jaffer, who would display the form, and cunningly insinuate the blasphemous arrogance of a fallen sinner's asserting a claim to a place in Heaven. He would explain to them, as he had explained to me, that the outrageous claim was an act of diabolical pride, proving the claimant forever unworthy of Divine Mercy. He would make it crystal clear that only an impenitent rebel against the Divine Will could sincerely put in a demand for transfer. The souls most discontented with the environment of Hell would be precisely those most likely to shrink from any new challenge to the manifest will of celestial authority. I was convinced now that, though the original regulation had been laid down in Heaven, the machinery for operating it had been cunningly devised in Hell. Devised in such a way as to deepen the despair of the wretched and plunge them forever in hopelessness.

Once I saw the problem clearly, I knew what to do. If the form was at fault, the form must be altered. I would use it, and yet say nothing to which I could not give an honest, rational and even humble assent.

This decision made, I returned quickly to the hotel, to see how I could execute it. In my lonely bedroom I took out the form and, for the first time, found myself able to contemplate it without acute misery. It was simple and straightforward on the surface. Yet I now knew that it was fashioned by devilish malice and cunning, and deserved to be treated accordingly.

Preliminary Application for Transfer to the Celestial
                          Kingdom
1. Name of Applicant ....
2. Federal Zone ....
3. Judgment given in Condemnation ....
4. Brief Statement of your reasons for making this application ....
   ....
   ....
   ....

I determined not to go one step beyond what could be justified. Having, therefore, filled in my name and zone, and inserted "NONE" in section 3, I did two things only. I crossed out "Transfer to the Celestial Kingdom" and substituted "Removal from Hell." And then I filled in section 4 with the only statement I could in conscience bring myself to make. "I hate Hell generally, and Jaffer in particular."

Half-afraid lest second thoughts might raise some

new and knotty problem, throwing all my plans into the melting-pot again, I hastily folded the form into an envelope, addressed it to the Foreign Office, and ran out of the hotel to the nearest post box. I did not encourage a single reflection until the thing was lost to me forever. And then I had the satisfaction of feeling—not that the application expressed all my desires, all that I willed for myself at the present juncture in this miserable situation, for it did not—but that it expressed the only aspiration which I could justifiably will myself to indulge. In short, it did not so much express my will as what, in my better judgment, I thought my will ought to be. I am no psychologist, but I think that my will became more nearly the same thing that I wanted it to be, as a result of this action. At any rate, I found myself, for the moment, less obsessed with my own spiritual state and the kind of treatment it deserved. Instead, my thoughts began to revolve around the severely practical problem of how to get away.

As I crossed the road from the post box, I saw two Powers standing on the steps before the door of the Information Bureau, and I immediately recognised them as Jaffer and Coffer. It was no good hoping that they might not see me, for they were both directly facing me, and Jaffer motioned me toward them.

"You are the very person we were talking about," he said. "You must come inside and have a chat."

They took me into the office, and gave me a seat and a cigarette. Coffer stood deferentially inside the door, while Jaffer sat, confidently and informally, on the edge of his desk.

"Coffer here has explained to me the irregularities attending your arrival here."

I nodded at Coffer, but the recognition did not disturb the uncomfortable coldness that marked the meeting of our eyes.

"It is an exceptional case," Jaffer went on, "and does not call for an inflexible application of our customary rule of procedure. I will go so far as to say that, in the circumstances, we might consider the unusual course of directly aiding you to obtain a transfer. That is, if you are still anxious to leave us—and are prepared to be reasonable."

I replied that I had not changed my mind.

"Well, then," said Jaffer, "we must put our heads together and see what can be devised."

Then, with a sudden jerk of the head, he turned to Coffer.

"He deserves some consideration, you think?"

"Some," said Coffer. "He certainly was prepared to help in checking up on the celestial spy."

I was thrown into confusion again. I could see that my behaviour might have disposed the Powers in my favour. But this very behaviour was the thing that made Hell right for me. It couldn't, surely, be the first grounds of hoping for escape.

"It may be just a question of finding the right formula," said Jaffer. "Sometimes these problems are solved more easily than one expects. It may well be that I can do the trick. That is, provided you don't mess things up yourself. You haven't applied for a celestial transfer, have you?"

He asked this question casually, so that I was able both to absorb the shock and to meditate a reply. I decided on a white lie. I hadn't applied for a celestial transfer. I had applied for removal from Hell.

"No," I said. "I changed my mind about that."

"That's a good thing," said Jaffer. "As I said before, nothing finally ruins a fellow in celestial eyes like a transfer application."

"However it is framed?"

It was a rash question; but I was both curious and apprehensive, and could not resist it.

"There's no way of getting round the thing. However you fill it up, it represents a claim which the Celestial Powers won't listen to. I remember a desperate fellow who thought he could send in an application sufficiently modest and unassuming to impress the Celestial Powers with his humility and submissiveness. So, in the statement of reasons for making the application, he wrote—'I'm not asking to get into Heaven. I merely want to get out of Hell. It's wicked and horrible.' I was working in the Foreign Office at the time. We laughed at this a good deal, but we forwarded it above, just to see what would happen. It came back with the usual official stamp—'REJECTED'—and this comment on it in red ink: 'Negative and unworthy of consideration. No indication of a single positive desire to serve the Powers Celestial.' "

Jaffer laughed gently and reminiscently at the end of this anecdote, and Coffer contributed a prolonged deferential smile. For myself, I was stunned, as by a physical blow. All my recently-established hopes crashed in dust around me. I tried at first to put on a smile adequate to conceal my discomfiture. But the screwing-up of my eyes and mouth, which resulted from the painful effort, was as plain a scowl of misery as ever I was conscious of producing. Moreover, I was aware of a burning scarlet blush, rising over my cheeks and forehead.

"Well, well," said Jaffer cheerfully, "it's easy for

some people to make mistakes, isn't it? No, no. Let me assure you that you were right to leave the form alone. It isn't any use at all to fill it up. It can't help you. If you can excuse an indiscretion on my part, I may say that it was never meant to help anyone. It's a trap for the unwary; and you were very wise indeed to give it a wide berth."

I shrank back into my chair, and my mind wriggled in torment. Jaffer's every word seemed to contain a bitter sting.

"I think," said Coffer, eyeing me in cool calculation, "that he can bear to hear the truth. It is not as though he had himself committed the blunder of sending in a form."

"Quite right," said Jaffer; and he looked me in the eyes. "You are a rational man. We must tackle this problem from the roots. And the first question we must ask is this: What are the Celestial Powers looking for, when they select their new entrants? The answer is simple. They are looking for a certain state of mind, which they call submissiveness. That alone interests them. How is this state of mind cultivated? It depends where you are. On the Earth, this state of mind is produced by an unconscious process. A man learns by all kinds of external influences and disciplines to submit himself to the celestial demands. This development happens in him while he is concentrating on quite other matters—quite irrelevant matters seemingly: how to feed and clothe his children; how to scrape together the money for an electric washing-machine to ease his wife's work; how to comfort a dying uncle, and so on. These things act as a secret discipline in self-surrender to the Other, which is alone what the Celestial Powers value. But this process can operate only in a community of interdependent persons. On the Earth, of course, all men dwell inevitably in community.

"In Hell the situation is different. This is not a community, but a society of individuals, passionately concerned for their own freedom and independence. Here, therefore, men cannot stumble upon an external discipline in submission by thinking about the needs of others. If you try to help a man here, he has sufficient self-respect to fling your interfering patronisation back in your face. You see, Hell is wholly inhabited by men of self-respect, who abhor the indignity of receiving charity at the hands of others. Nothing lowers a man in his own self-esteem like the insult of proffered assistance. Here, then, it is impossible for a man to lapse into that state of mind cultivated by the Celestial Powers, for the simple reason that he cannot here spend his time in the service of others.

"This makes it extraordinarily difficult—and, generally speaking, impossible—for the human inhabitant of Hell to attain to that state of submission which is a prerequisite for transfer to Heaven. The view of the Celestial Powers is that you were offered a comparatively easy road to the Kingdom while on Earth, and you refused to take it. Now your way is harder. So hard, as I have said, that it may generally be regarded as impossible."

Jaffer's statement was so clearly in accord with the truth that I could not but listen attentively. There was no doubt that he understood Hell—and that he understood the nature of the celestial demand too. My respect for his intelligence and grasp was further strengthened; and I waited eagerly to see what he would say in concluding the argument.

"Not quite impossible, however," he said, with an indulgent smile, "otherwise this interview would be meaningless. You are forced back upon the hardest route of all. Where you cannot learn submission by thinking about others, you must learn it by thinking about yourself. Few, very few, men have the spiritual capacity for conquering the self by concentrating on the self. It is not the way for men of common stamp. It is the way of heroes. And to this you must wind up your nerves and tighten your will. The easy way is closed. The external discipline of service to others is not available. You cannot slip into submission. You must *force* your way to Heaven, resolutely creating in yourself that state of submission which nothing here will assist you to fashion. You must endure the artist's agony of self-obsession. You must live your life from hour to hour in a fever of perpetual self-analysis and self-correction. Ever reflecting upon your own inner thoughts and desires, you must cut and hew your will to submission, as a sculptor rends the statue from granite. Nothing here will aid the work. Yet you must persevere, until you fashion an inner integrity of surrender, acceptable to Heaven. Alone, you must create your own passion of resolute submission, daily refining it of all contamination by the alien philosophy which permeates the very air you breathe.

"It is, as I said, the task of an artist. And you must never cease for a moment to think of the work upon which you are engaged. Yourself must be your only study, as you strive to create your greatest masterpiece of all—a self patterned within and without to the demands of your own soul's urgent need; a self cleansed of all extraneous interests and irrelevant preoccupations; a self stamped through and through with the single-hearted will to submit and be saved. You have got to make the purest thing you ever made, unsullied in its passionate integrity by the perversions thronging around you—the utterly devoted, utterly given, seven-times purified self; of your own devising, of your own fashioning, of your own cherishing; the product of your toil and the fruit of your torment; the one, true, pure, immortal sacrifice, ever, in His Mercy, accept-able unto Him."

"But this is impossible," I said. "It can't be done."

"It is weakness to shrink," said Coffer.

"I don't mean that it's difficult, when I say impos-sible," I cried in some consternation. "I mean that it's inherently impossible. The whole recommendation is self-contradictory."

"That may be so," said Jaffer, "but I warned you that it was a way for exceptional men only."

"For lunatics," I shouted. "Self-willed self-conquest is impossible. If it's self-willed, it isn't self-conquest; and if it's self-conquest, it isn't self-willed. The un-aided self can't will self-abnegation. You can't rely upon yourself in transcending self-dependence. You can't yourself create a sacrificed self; for the self that would do the creating is the self that has to be sacri-ficed. Language and logic are outraged in your ad-vice. It's nonsensical."

"But it's the only way," said Coffer.

"For Hell," said Jaffer, "is the domain of the self-re-liant."

"And you are in Hell," said Coffer.

"Hell is wholly inhabited by the self-dependent."

"And you are in Hell," repeated Coffer.

"There is no escape from self-service, where the at-tempt to escape is the greatest self-service of all."

"That is what Hell means," said Coffer.

"There is no refuge in submission, where the search for a refuge is the rebellion of the will."

"That is the nature of Hell," said Coffer.

"It's intolerable," I said, almost screaming the words, driven desperate by their oppressive iterations. "There must be something to turn to."

"There is nothing to turn to," said Jaffer. "For nothing exists here except isolated, unresponsive, independent selves; individuals who will take nothing and who can give nothing. For practical purposes, only the self exists."

"Were it not so," said Coffer, "it would not be Hell."

"There can be no self-disciplines where charities are impossible—"

"And where worship is self-indulgence."

"There can be no self-transcendence, when you are locked in an eternal isolation of self-hood."

"Which is what makes Hell Hell," said Coffer.

"On the Earth, you can flee to the Church in penitence."

"But here all penitence is self-seeking."

"On the Earth you can cry for mercy—"

"But here the cry is rebellion."

"On the Earth you can seek to nourish the soul by hearing the word, by sacrament and by prayer—"

"But here you are cut off from Grace—"

"Shut out from salvation—"

"Numbered among the dead."

"Stop, stop!" I cried, utterly overwhelmed by the pressure of their comminations. "If I can do nothing else, at least I can reject your teaching."

"You cannot even do that," said Jaffer.

"For rejection is impossible," said Coffer.

"And on your own showing. For the self that would reject is the self which cannot reject—"

"Being itself rejected."

"As the self that would repent is the self which cannot repent—"

"Being already condemned."

"As the self that would submit is the self which can never submit—"

"Having only itself to rely upon."

"Wherefore—" said Jaffer, rising suddenly to his feet, extending his two hands over my head, and intoning his words with awful solemnity—"Wherefore, O eminent Disposer of all our hearts, Thou to whom all our lives are yoked in the passionate pursuit of self-fulfilment in liberty, and Who hast taught us that a day in the free habitations of Hell is better than a thousand in the courts above, receive this thy servant into thine ardent keeping—"

"Defend him," said Coffer, "from all assaults of alien Powers."

"Protect him through the long night watches from all fruitless visitations of penitence or remorse."

"Be to him," said Coffer, "a pattern of self-motivated endeavour."

"Grant him to dwell within the shadow of thy wings, growing daily in the service of self; whom to serve is perfect freedom."

"Amen and Amen."

"And now," said Jaffer coldly, "you may go."

A Dream and its Sequel

Come, come away, fraile, feeble, fleshly wight,
Ne let vaine words bewitch thy manly hart,
Ne divelish thoughts dismay thy constant spright.
In heavenly mercies hast thou not a part?
Why shouldst thou then despeire, that chosen art?

SPENSER: *The Faerie Queene*

I dragged myself back to the hotel, inwardly given
over to desolation and despair. As I climbed the stairs
to my bedroom, a wave of faintness came over me,
and I remembered that I had had nothing to eat since
breakfast. In the excitement and activity consequent
upon the debate, I had missed lunch; and it was now
late afternoon. However, I think the spasm of faintness was a blessing in disguise. For, on entering my
room, I threw myself immediately on the bed, and
within five minutes all my present miseries were for-
gotten. I was fast asleep.

Distinct and significant dreams have been rarities
with me, and the few I have had stand out clearly in
my memory; but none so clearly as the dream that
came to me at that crisis of desolation. I was a child
again, spending a holiday at the familiar little cottage
which my father rented in the North Yorkshire hills. I
must not say exactly where it was, but anyone for
whom names like *Chop Yat*, *Roseberry Topping* and
Ingleby Greenhow carry definite pictures and distinct
associations, will know the immediate background of
steep curling lanes, little grey bridges and unexpected

watersplashes, and the remoter background of forested slopes and purple moors.

In my dream, I stood at the bedroom window, looking down on the waterfall at the bottom of the garden, and on the familiar stream which ran towards it through a winding gap in the fir trees, now lightly swaying in the autumn breeze. And I wondered, as I had so often wondered before, why the woods, which were so quiet during the day, moaned so incessantly when the darkness came to my silent bedroom. My mother came upstairs and tucked me into bed. Then she sat on the coverlet, opening the brown-backed book of stories from the *Faerie Queene*, which was always an especial favourite. I can remember its smell— but not, of course, its editor or publisher. I can remember the slight, yet richly coloured pictures of Archimago and the Cave of Mammon, but none of the phrases which brought these things to life.

This evening my mother read how the Red Cross Knight fought with the giant Gorgoglio and was imprisoned in a deep dungeon, and how the giant dressed the false Duessa in gold and purple, and enthroned her upon a seven-headed dragon. She read how the lovely Una brought Prince Arthur to the rescue, who slew the giant and the dragon, and set the tortured knight free. And lastly, she read how the Red Cross Knight encountered the ogre, Despair, in his cave, and could do nothing to counter his temptations, until Una urged him to run away. And here my mother closed the book.

"That's enough for tonight," she said. "The knight fought very bravely against Sans Foy and Sans Joy and Gorgoglio: but he was wise enough not to linger with

Despair and fight with him."

"Why not?" I asked.

"Because you can't defeat Despair in that way. One day you'll understand. You mustn't stay in the company of Despair. He's not someone you struggle with. He's someone you run away from."

Then, suddenly, my mother was gone from the dream. And there was darkness all around me in the lonely bedroom. Outside the wind moaned in the trees. And the stream below hissed ferociously, like the sea. And the spray from the waterfall flung itself into my bedroom and stung my face as it lay on the pillow. I shrank beneath the bedclothes, tingling and terrified. My feet felt cold and damp; and I knew that the waterfall was now pouring down the side of the house. I gripped the screwed-up ends of my blanket and cried out for my mother. And the effort jerked me, with a convulsive trembling, out of sleep.

The relief of finding myself free of the threat from wind and waterfall, and the sheer joy of not being a terror-stricken child in the darkness, made me feel positively heartened as the real situation dawned upon me. "Thank God!" I muttered, and then added, with a sigh, "And deliver me from this also!"

I stood up, pulled myself together, washed my face, and decided to go in search of a cup of tea. Coming downstairs into the entrance hall, it suddenly struck me that one cup of tea outside the miserable hotel was better than a thousand inside; so I walked out into the street.

Was there a message in my dream? Or did it not rather express my continual preoccupation with the desire to get away? I stared blankly across the street into the entrance to the Underground Railway which had first brought me to Hawk. I had thought so much about getting away. Had I really *tried* to get away? An idea, absurd in its simplicity, sent me running across the street into the Underground booking office.

"Central Lift Terminal," I said.

"You're not trying to get away?" asked the green bus conductor, warily.

"No fear!" I said, lying more cheerfully than I had ever lied before.

"Meeting someone?"

"That's it," I said, and the second lie was even more enjoyable.

But the train journey was a tedious torment. I was alone in the long carriage—perhaps the only passenger in the train. Yet I knew that on the return journey the carriages would be packed to capacity. Was not this fact alone a source of danger? How could an isolated traveller in the wrong direction escape the supreme suspicion?"

"Oh, God," I prayed, "get me out!"

And the train carried me through the darkness of the endless, winding tunnel, now sweeping evenly along the dead straight stretches, now straining and squeaking excruciatingly on the sudden bends. Sitting there in solitude, acutely sensitive to every variation in the direction of the train's course, down or up, to left or to right, I discovered that the underground path had the distinct and memorable vagaries of an overland road. For we curled this way and that way out of the city, then ran head first along an extended stretch. Several more bends brought a touch of variation, before we began to descend rapidly in a straight line. We swayed downwards, and the carriage rocked with easily-gathered speed. Then, suddenly, the train shuddered into a climb. And as we climbed, we made a wide sweeping turn to the left. Finally, a brief straight run brought us screeching to a standstill in the Central Lift Terminal.

I bounded from the train and careered through the white-tiled corridors, at first without proper aim, but soon guided by the detected rumble of the escalators. When I reached them, my way was barred by the bus conductor who was receiving a procession of newcomers.

"Wait a minute," he shouted to me. "You can't go up there!"

I gave him my ticket.

In lying, practice makes perfect; and perfection, I discovered, brings elation.

"Official business," I said. "No time to waste. The Director General has sent me to meet someone."

"Oh," he said.

And that was that.

All eight escalators were working in a downward direction; but they were far from crammed. And I discovered that to climb up a downward-moving staircase, though frustrating when progress is barred by obstacles in the shape of more orthodox passengers, brings with it a sense of triumph when successfully accomplished.

"Welcome to Hell," blared the loudspeakers, "the most misrepresented corner of the universe. Hell is fine. Hell is free. Its gates are open to all." Lifts screamed and gates clattered. People jostled and talked, and drifted down to receive their copies of the *Beginner's Guide*. Alone I sidled furtively up to the ring of gates. To add a final touch of dissimulation, I took out a notebook, referred to it, and ostentatiously surveyed the faces of arriving human beings. Then, as the shaft beside me disgorged its cargo, I neatly slid into the vacant lift, with so little time to spare that the crashing gate trapped the end of my jacket, and by the time I had torn it free, the lift had screamed the All-Clear and was soaring upwards.

Heavenly Company

As flames do work and winde, when they ascend,
So did I weave myself into the sense.
But while I bustled, I might heare a friend
Whisper, "How wide is all this long pretence!
There is in love a sweetness readie penn'd:
Copie out onely that, and save expense."

GEORGE HERBERT: *Jordan*

When the lift came to rest and the gate slid open, I found myself face to face with Lamiel, on the third story of the solicitors' offices.

"I was expecting you," he said gravely. "I may say that you are long overdue. What prevented you from taking an earlier train?"

This was a question which I found oddly difficult to answer.

"When I come to think of it," I said, reflectively, "I can't say what prevented me."

"You ought to think about it a little more intensely," said Lamiel. "And then perhaps it will occur to you that you alone prevented it."

"Really, that's harsh," I said. "I had no idea that it would prove so easy to get away."

"You got away as soon as you tried."

"I didn't think of trying."

"Then whatever were you engaged upon all the time?"

I laughed. It was the only thing to do. For what had I been engaged upon? Chiefly upon elaborate reflections on the fact that I wanted to get away and couldn't. It would sound absurd to present this as the thing that had so preoccupied me as to delay my actual attempt to escape.

"You haven't answered my question," Lamiel pressed.

"Very well, then, if you must have an answer. I didn't think of trying to get away, because I was too busy thinking of how to get away."

"Ah," said Lamiel. "Then it really was Hell."

"Indeed it was."

"No superlatives, please. You've only been in the suburbs."

"Then I shouldn't like to visit the metropolis."

"No, you wouldn't," said Lamiel.

"The place was wretched enough."

"You were very miserable?"

"Indeed I was."

"And conscious of your sinfulness?"

"Inevitably so."

"Then why didn't you prostrate yourself in penitence?"

This question too was a shamefully difficult one; and I was silent.

"You were too preoccupied?" asked Lamiel.

"Why, yes, I was."

"Reflecting," said Lamiel, "on the impossibility of penitence?"

"You know everything that I've been through."

"No," he said. "But I have a nodding acquaintance with the psychology of Hell."

"I think I have too, now."

"You always have had. But it is not the same as my own acquaintance with Hell's psychology."

I laughed again. Not that Lamiel's comments were uproariously funny. But laughter came very easily in my present frame of mind. Lamiel, however, continued to look grave; and I realised that he was expecting something.

"I'm sorry," I said. "I owe you an apology."

"You do," Lamiel agreed.

"I was treacherous, I know. It was partly sloppy thinking, and partly vanity."

"A good part vanity. Though there was certainly treachery. After all, I was your guest."

"And I was stupidly deaf to your warnings."

"You were," Lamiel agreed. "And you have suffered something in consequence."

"Yes," I said. "It was a revelation to me."

"You will be able to write another book."

"Oh, please, please!"

I waved a deprecating hand.

"Hell is very good box office."

The digs were unmistakable. I thought it best to respond playfully.

"Now, now," I said. "You shouldn't put ideas into my head."

"What would it contain," asked Lamiel, "if I didn't?"

Laughter bubbled up again. Lamiel was thundering good company at any time: after Hell, his very presence was heavenly.

We had now turned right up the High Street, and were walking towards my home.

"Even the faces of passers-by look different, I hope," said Lamiel, after some moments of silence between us.

"Yes," I said. "People look more approachable."

"They are approachable; provided that you make yourself available to them. But the great work must come first, of course. You will be so very busy with your writing."

The irony was heavy, and its general drift clear; but I missed its core.

"What exactly are you getting at?" I asked.

"You may be so busy pillorying individualism in solitude, that you won't have time for life in community."

"That sounds like Hell," I said.

"That is Hell. As you very well know. Or you ought to, now."

Again there was silence between us for a space. And then I brought out the question I most wanted to ask.

"Could anyone get out of Hell if he tried?"

"If he really tried."

"Which is not so easy as it sounds."

"Exactly. Trying to get away is quite different from thinking about getting away. Oddly easy, if the grace is granted. Otherwise the mere thinking stands in the way."

"The will doesn't operate, you mean?"

"No. It is too busy being 'free.' "

"You mean, its busyness in being 'free' is its servitude?"

"Precisely. And now perhaps you understand more fully why I approved, more than you did, the mere sight of people going to church—or rather, coming away from church."

"They weren't occupying themselves in being 'free'?"

"They weren't. Instead of thinking about their independence, they performed a simple operation of the will. They admitted their dependence. And to that extent became really free."

Something important dawned upon me: but it was too elusive to be clearly grasped and held.

"I think you're trying to tell me that getting into Heaven is like getting out of Hell."

"Not unlike at all. The thinking about getting into Heaven can be a great obstacle. But, if the grace is granted and the will begins to operate, forgetting for a moment to be 'free'—"

"If I go to church, you mean."

"Well, that is a start. That little duty will be a real freedom gained. But many more freedoms lie ahead— if the accumulating duties imposed after your submission are in turn fulfilled."

"More and more church-going?" I queried.

"Perhaps so. Perhaps just more and more reading to the children, or more and more washing-up. I don't want to moralise—still less to generalise."

"Perhaps even more and more writing?"

"Perhaps even that."

We reached the gate of my home, and Lamiel stopped.

"I leave you here," he said.

"You are going back?"

"Yes. I am going back."

"Oh," I said. And a new kind of sadness came over me.

"Shall I not see you again?"

Lamiel looked steadily at me.

"There is one point at which you will certainly see me again. That will be death indeed."

The words were unexpected, and I was shaken. I

laid my hand on the gate to steady myself.

"I quite understand," he said. "I don't expect you to look forward eagerly to that reunion. You are young yet."

It was comforting to hear him say so. I was beginning to wonder whether I was.

"Not," he added, "that there's anything to rely upon in that."

"No," I said pensively.

There was silence. I couldn't bring myself to say "Thank you." The words would sound ridiculously presumptuous. Various phrases expressing gratitude tumbled through my head, but they wouldn't do. So I just mumbled, "Good-bye."

"God be with you," he said simply, and turned from the gate to walk away. I stood still, overcome by the suddenness of his departure. After taking a few steps, he turned and smiled.

"I'm sorry about one thing," he called.

"What is that?"

He raised his hand in a final salutation.

"You haven't the right experience for a *Paradiso*!"